WIRED DAWN

PARADISE CRIME THRILLERS BOOK 5

TOBY NEAL

We are what we pretend to be, so we must be careful about what we pretend to be.

- KURT VONNEGUT, *Mother Night*

CHAPTER ONE

THE BOY RAN, stumbling in the darkness, toward the farthest black corner of the cave. His breath tore through his lungs. He put his hands out, slowing as the fire got further away, its flickering light dimming. The darkness thickened, and he tripped and almost fell on the loose, jagged stones of the cavern floor.

That voice like warm honey called his name. "Come, Nakai. What you running for? Where you think you can go?"

Nakai reached the back corner of the cave, a dark and drafty spot where he could feel fresh air welling like spring water from somewhere deep in the earth.

The man's footsteps approached, unhurried and confident. Nakai glanced back and saw his flashlight swinging, illuminating the harsh volcanic walls with every swing. "Stop this foolishness, boy."

Frantic, Nakai felt down the wall to the vent where the air came through. There was a small opening there, and he dropped to his knees and wriggled through.

Pitch darkness on the other side of the wall was thick as a muffling black blanket. Nakai crawled forward, biting his lips to keep from whimpering at the pain of rocks digging into his hands and knees.

"What, boy? You trying fo' get away?" That voice was the sound of evil disguised as a friend, the sound of the worst kind of betrayal. Even now, the boy's skin crawled at the memory of the man's hands on him—touching him, stroking and petting, pinching and forcing. "You want to leave so bad? You go, then. And sleep well in the dark."

Nakai stopped, holding his breath, turning back toward the slit illuminated by the flashlight's beam. He heard the scrape of a rock, and then the light blinked out.

He was in total darkness, and he was trapped.

Nakai turned and felt his way back in the direction from which he'd come.

Panic rose in a strangling wave and sweat burst out over his body as he crawled forward, and forward, and forward—and felt nothing ahead. No cleft, no wall. No light whatsoever.

He was lost in the dark already.

"Let me out! Help me!"

The stone seemed to vibrate around him, as if he sat on the head of a giant drum. "That's why music sounds so good in the cave," the man had told the circle of boys on Nakai's first night with the group of runaways. "This lava tube goes on for miles, and the porousness of the stone helps sound carry."

Maybe it would carry his calls for help. "Let me out!" Nakai cried again. "Help! I'm stuck in here!"

Nothing but the faintest echo of his terror came back to him.

Nakai crawled rapidly now, heedless of bleeding, determined to at least hit some kind of surface—and suddenly, he was out in space, falling into blackness that swallowed his scream.

CHAPTER TWO

SPECIAL AGENT MARCELLA SCOTT stood on a battered rubber mat outside the door of a shitty apartment on a run-down street in a bad part of Honolulu. The gritty zone of heat-shimmering concrete block buildings was sandwiched between the airport and a military installation, and the discordant sound of traffic going by on a nearby overpass competed with the wail of a police siren. The only evidence that the apartment was even in Hawaii was a battered and dusty plumeria tree on one side of the building. Its fragrant pinwheel blossoms sent up a waft of sweet scent. Marcella closed her eyes and breathed it in —and reached out and knocked.

No one answered.

She knocked again.

No answer.

Marcella dug in her pocket and brought out a thick bunch of keys. Her boyfriend, HPD detective Marcus Kamuela, always told her to thin them out. "You could do yourself an injury with that wad of keys," he teased. "Throw your back out carrying them, or at least bruise your ass sitting with them in your back pocket."

Marcella laughed, but didn't thin out the thick bunch of keys with its plastic New Jersey souvenir tag. *A girl had to remember where she was from.* Hence the cheesy key ring. Besides, Marcella loved keys. A key meant you were trusted, had access, and could get in.

She was the only person to have a key to this apartment besides its occupant.

Marcella flipped through the bunch: home, FBI office, parents' apartment, car, post office box, and on and on until she came to a couple of connected brass Schlage keys. Of course, just one wasn't enough for security conscious Sophie Ang.

Her friend Sophie had dealt Marcella a blow of betrayal that still had Marcella's temper flaring hot under her tidily buttoned blouse, if she thought about it too long.

And Sophie was likely holed up in there, blackout drapes drawn, deep in one of her depression cycles. Angry as Marcella was, *Sophie needed her.*

Marcella opened the thumb lock and with the other key, the deadbolt. She pushed the door inward. "Sophie?"

She felt the emptiness of the place instantly. Ginger, Sophie's energetic golden Lab, was absent. The apartment smelled stale and sour, but she called again, anyway. "Soph!"

No answer.

Marcella shut and locked the door. Sophie wasn't at her father's. Frank Smithson had been the one to call Marcella to go check on his daughter. "She has a three-day window to contact me, and it's been four days. You know how she gets, and where she hides," he'd told her this morning. "Can you go by her place?"

This bolt-hole of Sophie's was rented in the name of an alias, Mary Watson, and, as far as she knew, Marcella was literally the only one who knew where it was.

Marcella wrinkled her nose at the smell of garbage that had been left under the sink. She opened the refrigerator. Very little inside. She walked into the back bedroom. The bed Marcella and Frank had bought for Sophie was neatly made up—but the sense of emptiness persisted.

Marcella opened the closet and frowned.

The hangers were empty. She opened the drawers of the dresser. Nothing inside.

Sophie was gone.

Marcella straightened, heart rate spiking. She hurried now, whipping open the drawers of the desk looking for clues. Everything was removed but a notepad and some leftover office detritus: a few Post-its and pens, some tape. The monitor Sophie plugged into her high-end laptop when she was here was still there, but every personal anything that belonged to her friend was gone.

Would Sophie have run? Did she not trust the system that much?

The sound of a key at the entrance brought Marcella racing back into the front room, whipping the door open.

"Sophie!" Her friend's name died on Marcella's lips.

A short man with a greasy comb-over and a basketball of a belly straining a UH Rainbow Warriors jersey stood before her. Brown eyes blinked at her from behind thick glasses. His pidgin English was thick. "Eh, sistah. Whatchu doing heah?"

Marcella's hand had fallen automatically to the weapon at her side. "FBI. Who the hell are you?"

The man's eyes widened and he took a step back. "Building manager. I nevah know notting what dis renter was doing in heah."

Marcella took out her cred wallet and held it up for the man to see. "I need to know where the woman who rents this place is."

The manager's gaze darted up to the left. He was considering what to tell her, how much to lie. Marcella softened her voice and stance, opening her hands in appeal. "Sorry if I gave the wrong impression. The woman who lives here is missing and I'm looking for her. She didn't do anything wrong." *At least I hope not.*

"I nevah know notting," the manager whined.

Marcella's quick temper spiked. She shot out a hand and grabbed him by the wrist, yanking him inside the apartment. He stumbled across the threshold with a little yelp and she slammed the door behind him. "Where is she? Tell me now, or I'll take you in for questioning in her disappearance."

"She paid me for six months in advance!" the man burst out. "She said no tell anyone she lived here anymore. Said she was going to be in and out. Nevah said notting about no FBI!"

Marcella looked him over. Sweat had popped out in beads on his brow and upper lip. His gaze darted around the room.

He was telling the truth.

"Did she tell you where she was going?"

"No. Only that she liked her privacy."

So, Sophie had anticipated Marcella would come looking and paid this jerk to keep quiet about it. Anger rose in a hot flash.

"Get out of here," Marcella snapped. "And you better not rent this place out from under her. But if you see her, tell her the FBI is looking for her."

The man scrambled to the door and slammed it shut behind him.

Marcella took several deep breaths, trying to calm herself. *That bitch!* Some friend Sophie was, first holding back intel about the online vigilante she was dating, next pulling a disappearing act when she might be facing a murder charge! The situation Sophie faced and its consequences were dire, and leaving her father and friends hanging wasn't mature.

But maybe Sophie had never had the chance to grow up. She'd been trying too hard just to survive.

Marcella's gaze landed on a colorful postcard held onto the rusting, avocado-colored fridge with a magnet.

She walked over and removed a scene of the stunning Na Pali Cliffs on Kaua'i, their corrugated, jutting green expanse marching into a blue horizon like an endless row of Chinese clay soldiers. A caption in yellow at the bottom blared *Visit Kalalau!*

Marcella slipped the postcard into her pocket. She screwed up her nose at the foul-smelling garbage.

Who knew when Sophie would be back? It would be awful to come home to this reek.

Marcella pulled the white trash can liner out of the plastic can, tying it tight, and looked around one last time. "I'm going to find you, Sophie," she muttered. "You can run, but you can't hide."

She carried the trash out and locked the door behind her.

CHAPTER THREE

Sophie folded her damp tent as tightly as she could, but still, somehow, the damn thing had expanded. She usually had to refold it several times before she could get it back into its tight nylon bag, and the ever-present, bright red Kaua'i mud adhering to the slick plastic bottom made her hands and knees filthy.

"No one told me how dirty you get camping," she remarked to Ginger. The Lab looked on, tongue lolling in her usual doggy grin. Sophie had taken to talking to Ginger as days went by without other human contact.

There had been other hikers on the trail to Kalalau, of course. She and Ginger had done the rugged eleven-mile hike in two segments as she got used to carrying the heavy pack and working her camp stove, water filtration system, assembling and breaking down her tent and gear. She'd sent her obligatory text on the third day to her father, letting him know she was still alive, but her phone revealed *No Signal.*

"That Lyft driver said it was ambitious to take on Kalalau as a first-time backpacker," Sophie said, scrunching the tent down tightly. "I think he might have been right." Ginger woofed in agreement. The

Lab's coat was rough with mud; it had rained off and on for the five days they'd been out here. "Maybe it will be drier deeper inside the valley if we can find a ridge to shelter behind."

Finally wrestling the filthy tent into its packet, Sophie finished breaking camp and brushed soil and leaves over her fire ring. She'd camped near the stream since she finally arrived at the remote valley, with its famously stunning, jungle-clothed ridges that opened from a peak at Kokee and spread into a wide, lush valley that ended at a massive beach and the wide blue sea.

But the beach was populated with other campers and frequented daily by boatloads of tourists who came via Zodiac from Port Allen on the south coast. Sunburnt and loud, their juice boxes and sandwiches and snorkel gear celebrated a vacation in paradise...but Sophie wasn't here for a vacation.

She wasn't entirely sure why she was here, except that she had needed to get away and start a new chapter in her life. The postcard she'd found in the Ghost's apartment had drawn her here with the extreme beauty of this setting.

She'd fled Oahu and the remains of her life. Fled a broken heart, a possible murder charge, and even her own pattern of falling into a black hole of depression.

So far, the crazy idea had worked to keep her demons at bay. Hiking and learning to survive outdoors all day had been a total distraction: she was too tired by nightfall to wonder or worry, happy just to burrow into her tiny tent with her dog, and sleep the deep and uncomplicated sleep of the physically exhausted.

The depression medication might be working, too. This was the first time in her life she'd resorted to the stuff, but the circumstances had dictated a radical intervention. She had a three-month supply, and hopefully, she'd be ready to resume a normal life by the time her prescription ran out.

Or maybe not.

Sophie popped the little white pill into her mouth and swished it down with a mouthful of water she'd filtered and boiled from the nearby stream. "Come, girl. Let's go."

Ginger fell in behind Sophie as she pushed ahead, thankful for her wet-dry hiking shoes because the narrow trail was slick with iron-rich red mud, winding between tall banks of pili grass, and wild guava trees. The smell of wet grass, mold, and the sweetness of rotting fruit flavored the air. Sophie plucked a yellow guava off one of the trees and bit into it as she pushed forward, already feeling the forty-pound pack's weight sinking heavily onto her hips. She paused to tighten the belt so that the weight didn't land on her lower back.

She took another bite of the firm, tangy guava, enjoying the sweet-sour pink flesh as she paused to look around at the soaring, green-robed sides of the valley. This place reminded her of Waipio Valley on the Big Island, her first real exposure to this environment —and a case that had scarred her for life.

Sophie shut down the memory of that place, that case—and of her partner Jake, who'd saved her life.

Jake Dunn.

She wouldn't think of him, of her conflicted feelings about and toward him. Because thinking of him reminded her of Connor. And Connor didn't deserve anything from her, at all. She was off men. *Forever.*

Sophie hurried, bumping into Ginger and urging the dog into a trot. She used the sturdy bamboo stick she'd picked up on the first day she left to push branches out of the way and for leverage as she hiked as rapidly as physically able, straight toward the back of the valley.

She'd heard from some other hikers that there was some kind of settlement back there, a village of renegade local people who refused to honor the five-day permits issued by the state for camping. She was ignoring the five-day limit too, and thus needed to avoid areas patrolled by state park rangers.

The trail meandered along a clear stream, climbing steadily back toward the steep head of the valley where the junction of the walls boasted a waterfall that plummeted hundreds of feet.

Sophie paused eventually to let Ginger drink from the stream and to drink herself, from a canteen of boiled water. At each elevation, she paused to look back at the view down toward the ocean, to savor a slight breeze that dried away sweat brought to the surface of her skin by effort and humidity.

Sophie wanted to see the waterfall, and then she'd pick another campsite. One with enough openness that hopefully she'd get her gear dried out, and be able to connect her satellite-ready laptop with some satellite internet.

She hadn't been online for five days, an eternity for someone as "wired in" as she was normally. After the first couple of days of free-floating anxiety, she'd come to enjoy the anonymous feeling of being unplugged.

She was well and truly off the grid.

And she'd left everything and everyone behind—including her name and identity. Her father. Her partner Jake. And her friends Lei and Marcella.

It was all the Ghost's fault. *That bastard had let her grieve for him…*

Sophie shook her head to rid it of buzzing, painful thoughts as she reached a small knoll surrounded with the bright yellow-green of kukui nut trees in full leaf. The remains of *lo'i*, the ancient Hawaiian terraces used in the cultivation of taro, provided a stacked rock wall that would block the wind. If she was under the trees, her camp would be out of the sun. She could set up camp now and see the waterfall later…but she didn't want to be in sight of the path.

"Come, Ginger." Sophie turned off the trail and bushwhacked through waist-high ferns and undergrowth deep into the grove of kukui trees.

Looking up into their interlaced branches, she enjoyed the hum of the wind blowing across the trees' large, palmate leaves. "This seems like a good spot."

She had just unslung her heavy pack, lowering it to the ground, when she heard the sound of gut-wrenching weeping. A woman burst through the bushes, making Ginger sit up and bark.

"Help me! My son is gone!"

CHAPTER FOUR

HE'D LOST HER.

The Ghost's fingers tapped his keyboard in a blur of motion. A sense of panic tightened his chest as he routed the surveillance cameras at the Kaua'i airport through another scrub program. Sophie's makeup had fooled the facial recognition, but by tracking Ginger instead, he hoped to spot her eventually.

The video feed caught Sophie and Ginger getting into a car with a strange driver at the baggage claim of the Kaua'i airport. The Ghost zoomed in on the license plate. Likely a ride-share vehicle, but in a few moments, he would know for sure.

He sat back in his chair, releasing a tense breath.

Sophie had taken the suggestion he'd planted and gone to Kaua'i.

When he'd pinned the postcard to her side of the desk at the hidden office they'd called the "Batcave," he'd hoped she'd pick up on the subliminal message he'd left her. There was a lot that demanded the Ghost's attention in that remote valley, and Sophie could be his eyes and ears.

But she had stripped herself, her clothing, and all of her possessions of the various tracking devices he had installed in and around her. She was too wary, savvy, and sensitive not to have noticed if he'd tried to plant a subdermal tracker on her. He'd slipped a harmless radioactive isotope into her tea that last time they'd been together in Paia. That would last a while, but was only detectable at a much closer range.

The Ghost had always hoped she would become his partner in the mission, but he had not anticipated falling in love with her. Emotion was a sickness in his bones, sapping his strength, draining his vitality and weakening the hunger for justice that had been fuel for so long. *He'd almost given up the whole game for her!*

Now, Connor just missed her with a longing that had not lessened since they parted at her Mary Watson apartment on Oahu.

He kept hoping to feel better, to reclaim his motivation. Even seeing the evidence that his manipulation to send her to Kaua'i had worked only tortured him with visions of hiking with her, Ginger and Anubis all the way to that remote and beautiful paradise to right wrongs.

But Sophie had rejected him even after he'd given her a copy of the Ghost software to pique her interest. She continued to cling to ineffective and outmoded methods of conventional legal action.

Connor's inability to execute Sophie's husband Assan Ang stuck in his craw. The one time he'd really needed to mete out justice on behalf of a worthy victim he loved had failed. He'd been too caught up in dealing with his own staged death and its aftermath to help Sophie when she really needed him.

Fortunately, she had dealt with Assan Ang herself.

Unfortunately, that had left her legally vulnerable.

That was unacceptable.

Perhaps he could at least help her with something. He scowled at the screen, and leaned forward in concentration, his fingers flying.

CHAPTER FIVE

NAKAI'S BREATH blasted out of him as he hit bottom.

The boy lay stunned in a blackness so thick that it felt like a weight against his eyes. Was he dead?

But dead people didn't feel pain, did they?

Nakai opened his eyes. At least he was fairly sure he opened his eyes, but there was no change in the oily density that surrounded him. He sat up slowly, surprised that he could move his arms and legs, that he had landed on something relatively soft in the harsh raw lava environment of the underground tube.

He didn't know how far he had fallen.

His thoughts scattered, like tiny, flashing fish in a tide pool, then re-formed, rushing at him in a burst of terror.

Why hadn't he just died? He was just going to, anyway, but now it would take a while and be painful and terrifying.

He smoothed his hands over rounded pebbles and noticed, for the first time, the sound of trickling water.

CHAPTER SIX

MARCELLA GOT into her black Honda Accord, turned on the air conditioning, and called Frank Smithson with the news about Sophie. "She's gone. Cleared out of her apartment, but rented it by paying cash for another six months."

"Why would she do that? She might be facing a murder charge!" Smithson's deep, resonant voice went taut with anxiety. "Sophie knows better than to run at a time like this!"

"I don't know why she ran, Frank." Calling the dignified ambassador by his first name felt uncomfortable, but Sophie's father had insisted she do so. "Sophie is desperate to put these events behind her. Maybe she decided she didn't want to go to jail for Assan, no matter what the DA decided." Sophie had killed her ex-husband in a brutal way. Assan Ang was a sadistic brute, and he had been torturing their mutual friend Lei, using her as a hostage to leverage Sophie into giving herself up. Killing Assan the first chance she got was the only sane and reasonable choice. The fact that he'd been unarmed at the time was merely semantics—he'd been armed in other ways.

"When will we know if the DA is bringing charges against her?" Frank asked.

Marcella, looking up through the windshield at the ugly building and its lone plumeria tree, shook her head. Belatedly she remembered that Frank couldn't see her gesture. "I'm supposed to go on record in a deposition today. I'm worried because I'm sure Sophie is supposed to come in as well." Marcella blew out a breath. "I'll try to hold them off for as long as I can, but if they find out she's gone…"

"That will not help her situation," Frank said. "We need to alert her employer, Security Solutions, and Jake Dunn, that partner of hers. Maybe they can locate her."

"Already on it. Don't worry, Ambassador. We'll find her." Marcella wished she felt as confident as her words sounded as she ended the call and pulled out, heading toward her office downtown in the Prince Kuhio building in Honolulu.

Her thoughts turned to the man most likely to know where Sophie was: a man whose memorial they'd recently attended together, but quite possibly very much alive.

Sheldon Hamilton, aka Todd Remarkian, had been Sophie's boyfriend—and also, according to Sophie, the cyber vigilante known as "the Ghost."

The Ghost, whatever his name was, had outsmarted all of them.

And with his computer skills, Marcella couldn't see Hamilton just letting Sophie disappear without any idea of where she'd gone. Marcella had no idea where Hamilton was or how to contact him. But the acting head of his company might know.

Marcella used voice command to call Kendall Bix, acting President of Operations at Security Solutions. She could hear the frown in Bix's voice when she told him she couldn't find Sophie at her last known address. "Of course we will try to locate her. Was there any evidence in her home pointing to where she might have gone?"

"No." But Marcella's fingers touched the postcard in her pocket. Could it be a clue? She only knew one person well on Kaua'i, but real estate developer and MMA fighting coach Alika Wolcott was someone Sophie had dated, and things had ended sadly between them. She couldn't bother the man on such a thin shred of information. "I have to give a deposition about the killing of Assan Ang. I hope to sound out the DA about any charges against her."

"Keep us informed. I will reach out to Jake Dunn and see if he has any information on her whereabouts," Bix said.

Marcella navigated the busy downtown Honolulu streets easily, headed for her parents' little Italian restaurant on a side street in Waikiki near the yacht harbor. She'd ordered several of her mother Anna Scatalina's popular meatball sandwiches for the office. "Oh good. Let me know if he knows anything. And I'd like to speak to Sheldon Hamilton regarding this matter. Do you have a contact number for him?"

A long pause. Clearly Bix was reluctant. "He's asked me not to give out that information. I would need a…subpoena."

"Really?" Marcella's already frayed temper exploded. "What the hell is he hiding?"

"I can't speak to that. He's just been through the tragedy of his best friend's death and is grieving…"

Marcella pulled her Honda onto the small side street leading to her parents' restaurant and mercifully found a parking space. "You're kidding, right? This guy goes missing, turns up for a dramatic announcement that he's living abroad permanently, dumps the business on Todd Remarkian, and then surfaces after his partner's death only to disappear again? This doesn't strike you as bizarre? Indicative of criminal behavior? Because that's what it says to me, buddy."

"I really couldn't say." Bix sounded like an English butler confronted by dog shit on the front stoop. "There has been no criminal activity that I'm aware of. In fact, we are Security Solutions, in business to prevent crime."

"Just give me his freakin' number or I'll come in, not just with a subpoena but with a team to turn your desks upside down looking for that cyber vigilante that we never found, but who is associated with your firm. And who knows? The raid might get leaked to the press." Marcella jumped out of the car and slammed the door, pissed off and glad to have somewhere to direct the frustration that was, at least in part, about Sophie.

"I don't take kindly to threats," Bix said frostily. "But we are ever mindful of keeping a good relationship with the FBI. You can reach him at this number." He rattled off a series of digits and ended the call.

Marcella hurried across the narrow side street just opposite the Waikiki Yacht Harbor with its flotilla of gently rocking sailboats, and into the Hawaii Italian Bistro. She sucked in a deep and restorative breath of the restaurant's aroma of basil, garlic, and fresh hot bread. The restaurant was mostly empty, between breakfast and lunch shifts. Her parents, retired from her father's successful shoe import business in Jersey, had drawn the line at offering dinners, too. She loved the traditional decorating: red tablecloths and bent-backed chairs contrasted with black and white checked flooring.

"'Cella!" Anna Scatalina's musical voice called from behind the glass case of cannoli and tiramisu. "These subs are getting cold and soggy. You know I don't like to have them go out anything less than our best."

Marcella advanced across the restaurant and took the paper sack from her mother after a quick kiss on both cheeks. Anna looked adorable in her chef's hat and an apron emblazoned with *Kiss the Cook*. "My bad, Mama. The guys love your hoagies no matter how cold they are. Where's Papa?"

"Down at the Yacht Club with his buddies, playing cards. He says he earned a break between shifts." Anna's lips pinched together in disapproval. "I keep telling him to stop the gambling, but he keeps winning."

"Hey, Marcella." Gustavo, dressed to wait tables today in a white shirt and black pants, poked his head out of the kitchen. "Did you think about my proposal?" The young Italian man was a distant cousin, as were most of the wait staff and kitchen helpers. There was always another relative from the Old Country who wanted to come to Hawaii to work.

"Dude, give it up," Marcella said. Gustavo had theatrically asked for her hand the first day he saw her. "You just want my mother's cooking. Permanently."

He clutched his heart. "Give me credit for knowing a good thing when I see it."

Marcella and her mother both laughed as Gustavo withdrew back into the kitchen and splashing sounds commenced. Anna narrowed her big dark eyes. "Speaking of marriage. When is that boyfriend of yours going to make an honest woman of you? Your papa, he doesn't like you shacking up."

Marcella had recently moved into a little cottage outside of Honolulu with Detective Marcus Kamuela of the HPD. They were blissfully happy, except when bothered by his Hawaiian mama or her Italian one to get on with marriage and children.

"Mama. Seriously. Give it a rest." Marcella tossed a twenty on the counter. "Or you'll never get grandbabies, and that's a promise."

"You're not getting any younger, 'Cella, and neither are we!"

Marcella scowled and grabbed the bag. "It's none of your business, Mama. Marcus and I love each other and that's enough for us." She spun and strode out the door. Only the customers present kept her mother from yelling after her in that crazy fishwife way that got activated whenever the subject of Marcella's future came up.

But heading for the door, Marcella felt a twinge of something like pain in the area of her ovaries. The clock was ticking, and she felt it too.

CHAPTER SEVEN

SOPHIE DROPPED the tent she had been unrolling and caught the distraught woman by her arms. "Slow down. Something happened to your son?"

Dark-haired with ashy brown skin, the woman was as thin as a methamphetamine addict, her eyes bloodshot and rolling in her sallow face. She collapsed in Sophie's arms, and Sophie lowered her gently to lie on the soft leaf mulch under the kukui nut trees. Ginger whimpered anxiously and crowded close, trying to lick the woman's face, but Sophie pushed the dog back. She unscrewed the top of her canteen and poured water into her palm, splashing it onto the woman's face and narrow, bony chest.

The woman came around from her faint, eyes fluttering open. Sophie lifted her upright and poured water into her open, gulping mouth. As soon as she was sputtering, Sophie took the canteen away and lowered her back down. "Just catch your breath. You must be dehydrated."

"Who cares? My son! My Nakai is gone!"

"Tell me your name."

"Enola."

"My name's Sandy. Sandy Mason." Sophie almost stumbled over the alias. "Why don't you start at the beginning? What happened?"

"My son ran away." Enola looked up, rheumy eyes defensive. "He's thirteen. Teenagers get in moods."

"I can imagine." Sophie kept all expression out of her face and voice. *It couldn't be easy having a druggie mother.* "So you are alarmed that he ran away?"

"Not so much that. I know where he went. He joined the lost boys at the top of the valley." Enola gestured toward the steep cliffs to the south. "The Shepherd looks after them. But he ran away from the Shepherd, too. Shepherd thinks something happened to him, that he got lost in the caves." Her voice caught and she covered her face with her hands.

Sophie was unsure where to start. "Why isn't this person helping you find your son?"

"The Shepherd helped me by taking him in. He helped me by telling me what he thought happened to Nakai." Enola struggled to her feet. "I have to get to the beach and get the police, the fire department, get someone to help find him!" She tore away from Sophie, staggering into the brush, heading for the trail.

Sophie frowned. What could she do for some lost child in an unknown cave?

Nothing. She could not do anything that would draw attention to herself in her current circumstances.

The strange situation of runaways living in a cave with a "shepherd" and a lost runaway would have to be dealt with by someone else.

CHAPTER EIGHT

NAKAI CRAWLED toward the sound of water. His hands and feet and knees, uncovered in the swim trunks he wore, were battered and bruised as he reached the trickle of an underground stream. He plunged his hands into the water, heedless of the burning of his palms, and scooped the liquid up to his mouth.

His thirst finally slaked, he sat back on his heels. The dark was just as complete as ever. In fact, there was no way to know exactly what he was doing, let alone have any idea where he was, without completely forgetting his sense of sight.

But he could survive with the presence of water. He remembered reading in health class before his mom pulled him out of school to go live in the valley: "Humans can only survive for around three days without water. But they can live a good long time without food."

Hope swelling his chest felt almost painful, like circulation returning after a leg had fallen asleep. He would be fine without food for a while, now that he had water.

Nakai shut his eyes because they were useless. Panic and fear were useless, too, and might even make him hurt himself, as he almost had, falling off the cliff.

Nakai stilled himself and really listened.

The sound of the water definitely started in one direction, and went in another. If the water was flowing, there must be a way out. *Maybe he could get out the same way the water did.*

Nakai had a sense of the spaciousness of the lava tube by the way the water's sound bounced around and vibrated inside the cave. He'd get better and better at being able to judge distance with just his ears alone as time went by. He would focus on that. He was a blind man now, and blind men got around just fine.

Nakai felt the ground, touching the pebbles lining the water area. They were a softer, gentler surface and could help guide him as he moved around.

"I am blind. But blind people find their way. Blind people live full lives. I am fine." Nakai's voice echoed a little, and that told him that there was still a lot of space around his spot. He shouldn't wander from the pebble bed and the stream. "Water is life." He reached into the water and felt the direction it was flowing, and began to crawl slowly beside it.

He muttered at first, talking to himself. "I can feel the edge here…I think I'm headed downhill. Where this water goes I can go." It was a lie, but he wanted to believe it. When he ran out of things to say, the silence felt as smothering as the blackness, so he began to sing.

He sang and he crawled, and he sang more and crawled further. He took a drink, curled up and rested a while, and then sang and crawled until he couldn't anymore.

CHAPTER NINE

AGITATED by Enola's disruptive visit, Sophie could no longer settle down to setting up her camp in the spot she had chosen. There were still several hours of daylight left; it couldn't harm anything to go further back into the valley and see what she could see.

She wasn't investigating, no. But if Sandy Mason happened to see or hear something to help, that wouldn't be a terrible thing, would it? Besides, she had a dog with a good nose. If Ginger could pick up the boy's scent, she might be able to help find him.

Before she even realized that she'd made a conscious decision, Sophie had rigged up her backpack and was back on the trail, heading further into the valley toward the steep, rugged, drip-castle peaks that defined the apex of Kalalau.

Both she and Ginger were soon panting as they tackled the steep trail, studded with black volcanic rocks and slippery with nightly rainfall that turned the dirt to a red clay slurry. Clouds collected against the precipitous canyon walls, and soon a light rain misted down on her and Ginger, cooling them as it wetted Sophie's clothing and hair, further matting Ginger's muddy coat.

Sophie passed several offshoots of well-trampled path heading into groves of kukui nut and native *hala* trees, a form of pandanus that the Hawaiians used for basketry, canoe sails, roofing, and floor coverings. Sophie had seen many examples of intricate weaving using the humble-looking tree's long, fibrous, spiny-edged leaves at the Bishop Museum on her date with Connor.

Hiking was meditative: a time when her mind mulled over the past, present, and future, but without the negative spirals that usually characterized times when she reflected alone and that led to her crippling episodes of depression.

Connor.

She tried to force the memory of his sea-blue eyes gazing into hers out of her mind. He'd betrayed her. Lied to her. *Let her grieve him.*

She was finished with him.

But with her ex-husband, Assan, gone from the picture, she was truly free. She didn't have to worry about that specter waiting to pounce on her and anyone she showed an interest in.

But she was done with men. Her judgment clearly couldn't be trusted! First, she'd married a sadistic sociopath, then she'd fallen for a devious, brilliant liar with a relentless agenda.

But what about Alika Wolcott? Her former MMA coach's smiling brown eyes appeared in her memory. She'd been on the right track with her relationship with Alika. His muscled body, the way his black hair waved off his brow, the bold tribal tattoos on his arms, his confident moves in the ring were all impressed upon her. His challenging teaching and steady friendship had been authentic. Their heady kisses, unforgettable. Her only regret was that it had taken so long for them to even get that far.

Sophie was on Alika's home island, Kaua'i, and of course that would remind her of him.

Assan had almost killed Alika for the simple fact that Sophie had kissed him. Cared about him. Wanted to love him. Alika had chosen to leave to protect them both. She couldn't do anything about any of it; he no longer responded even to a text message from her. *But if he had, would she have gotten involved with Connor?*

It was hard to know the answer to that now. Maybe she could have spared herself heartache if Alika had given her any reason to hope, but he had chosen a clean break instead.

And she'd chosen the Ghost, and signed herself up for a world of hurt. She only hoped Connor was suffering a little too, *the two-headed offspring of a mutant goat!* He'd chosen his vigilantism over her and let her believe he was *dead!* She'd never forgive him, never let that go, never trust him again.

Trust. Jake's face rose to take Connor's place in her mind's eye. Her partner must be anxious that she'd disappeared. "He's freaking out," she could hear Marcella saying. "For God's sake, woman, tell him something or he'll drive us all nuts." But she hadn't so much as texted him.

Sophie banished that guilt. She didn't owe Jake anything. He might have had feelings for her at one time, but she was not responsible for that. She had never encouraged him, and now he was involved with Antigua, the lovely and talented chef and property manager at rocker Shank Miller's estate in Wailea.

They'd both made choices, and with Sophie's usual curse, she had chosen the wrong man. *Again.*

Next time she went out with someone, let alone slept with him, she'd ask her friends to choose for her! She almost smiled at the thought of Lei and Marcella hashing over her choices and making their best recommendations.

Who would they choose for her?

A moot point. She was done with men! *"A pox on all their asses!"* Sophie muttered aloud in Thai.

She hiked harder to get away from the buzzing noise of her thoughts, but Ginger gave a short, sharp yap that brought her out of her unpleasant reverie. They'd reached another kukui grove, this one in a wide, flat area. A path led off to the left, toward the trickling sound of the stream.

"Okay, girl. Let's go look." They walked down the path and Sophie spotted a knot of plastic-and-bamboo dwellings, hidden from the trail behind the broad, dark green leaves of small *noni* trees and the bigger, palmate-leaved *ulu*, or breadfruit trees. A ring of red *ti* leaf plants grew around the makeshift village, and though Sophie slowed, craning her neck to see if anyone was around, the place appeared deserted.

Perhaps they hid from strangers? But surely, they could see that she was no ranger or police officer, here to demand that they tear down their non-permitted dwellings...

Sophie studied the little village a moment. The houses were built of logs and branches nailed to living trees, with clear plastic walls. Roofs were made of heavy duty tarps pitched at an angle to allow water to roll down and off the crude dwellings.

Probably the villagers were nearby, watching her. She didn't want to give them cause for concern.

"Come, Ginger." Sophie tweaked the Lab's leash and continued past the encampment, feeling a sense of relief as she did so—there was an oppressive feeling about the place.

Sophie eventually reached a spot she liked: a small native *noni* tree grove with a clear area in the middle of the trees and thick, concealing leaves to the ground that gave her a feeling of protection and privacy. She didn't want any more disturbing incidents like Enola staggering into her peaceful camp.

She erected her deep green tent, pleased with how the camou-flage fabric blended with the leaves and undergrowth. She went back out to the trail to try to spot it, and could not.

By then the light was going, and Sophie was too tired to make a fire. She had a quick wash in the chilly stream, rinsing away the sweat of the day with biodegradable soap, then made a simple meal of dehydrated bean protein and vegetables on her camp stove. Sitting on a rock above the stream, watching the sky toward the sea go salmon and gold, Sophie ate her dinner, then wrapped her arms around Ginger's neck and felt gratitude sweep through her.

She might be on the run from a murder rap for killing her ex. She might be alone, an unknown in an unknown land. She might be nursing a broken heart and traveling under an assumed name, not even sure who she was anymore—but right now, she was in a beautiful place, with a loving dog, and she had no one to account to for the first time in her life. No one to tell her what to do, who to be, where to go. No rules, no schedule, nothing but nature all around her.

Freedom was a sweet elixir she drew in deeply with every breath. She shut her eyes and leaned her head upon Ginger's back.

She heard something.

A faint human voice singing a song in Hawaiian.

And it was coming from the very rocks around her.

The hairs on Sophie's body rose as "chicken skin" broke out over her. Was this *mana,* the spiritual power Hawaiians claimed indwelled the trees, rocks, and very substance of the world? Could the singer be a *Menehune,* one of the legendary little people no longer seen in the Islands?

Fanciful thoughts. There was a reasonable explanation.

Sophie stayed very still and listened closely, seeking directionality, a source. Ginger's ears were pricked, her eyes bright as she whined deep in her chest. The dog heard it too.

Off to the left.

Stealthy and silent, Sophie unwound her arms from around the dog. She crept forward, closer and closer to a rock formation, an unprepossessing pile of boulders that seemed to be the source of the sound. She reached the black stones, worn smooth by annual floodwaters and the elements.

The singing was louder here, the clear, high voice that of a child, and Sophie smiled as she recognized "Hawaii Pono'i," the state song.

Sophie circled the rocks but could find no opening where anyone could be hiding. She couldn't see a source of the strange amplification.

And then, abruptly, the song ceased, and the silence felt like loss.

CHAPTER TEN

MARCELLA TUCKED her neat white button-down shirt into the black gabardine dress pants she preferred for work at the FBI, her round, rebellious breasts strapped down into a no-nipple-show breastplate of a bra. Her personal indulgence, designer shoes, were limited today to a pair of conservative bronze Ferragamo pumps that peeked from beneath the hem of her slacks and gave her a little boost of confidence. She touched up her lipstick, made sure her hair was tight in its businesslike twist, and headed into the conference room at the district attorney's office where she was to give her deposition regarding the death of asshole extraordinaire Assan Ang.

Marcella's union rep, a well-turned-out young man wearing a Harvard tie, was already seated. He stood and extended a hand. "Kyle Lovett. FBI Legal Counsel." Marcella shook his soft hand briefly.

Honolulu's new district attorney, rumored to be sharp and ambitious, was a small Chinese man named Chang with friendly wrinkles surrounding bright, cold eyes. They exchanged introductions, but the DA never offered his hand.

So that's how it was gonna be. Marcella met Chang's beady

bright stare. "I hope this won't take long. I have actual cases that need my attention."

"That is entirely up to you." Chang had a tic-like smile that revealed bright white veneers. "We all have priorities, and mine is to determine whether or not the slaying of an escaped federal prisoner was justified."

"I assume you have read over the case file," Marcella said, "because it is extensive." She sat and crossed her legs, lacing her fingers around a knee and keeping her expression neutral with an effort. "My friend and fellow agent has been through enough trauma as it is."

"I assume you mean *former* agent? I believe Sophie Ang is now what we call a freelancer, a mercenary in the security business. But let's get through the formalities before we begin, shall we?"

Marcella's neck flashed hot at Chang's dismissive tone. She inclined her head.

The DA switched on a wall-mounted video camera, stated the date, time, people present, purpose of the interview, and pushed a small black audio recorder toward Marcella. "Please tell us what you know about the relationship between Sophie and Assan Ang."

"I have known Sophie for around five years, since she first escaped from her sadistic torturer ex-husband, Assan Ang, and joined the Bureau," Marcella fired her words like bullets. "That Ang's death is even being considered anything but self-defense is ludicrous."

"Let's refrain from judgmental statements about the victim." Chang's cold eyes had narrowed.

"You told me to tell you what I knew about the couple's relationship. I have known Sophie for five years, as I said, and in all that time I have never seen or heard of Sophie interacting with her ex-husband except for occasions of trying to hide from him, escape him, or fight him off his deadly attacks toward her or toward people she cared about." *There was a special place in hell reserved for monsters like Assan Ang, with a frying pan set to eternal sizzle.*

Chang refused to meet her eye, instead making little squiggles on a notepad. She leaned forward to eyeball them and recognized Chinese. She could smell the sexism on this jerk, a funky aroma like old cheese—because she had boobs, he didn't take her seriously.

She had to calm down and stay objective or the DA would dismiss her testimony as biased hysteria. Marcella breathed out her anger and flicked at a bit of lint on her pants leg. "The few things Sophie told me about Ang and her marriage to him in Hong Kong were...terrible."

Marcella had difficulty finding a word that captured the horror Sophie had described in that flat, understated way she used when talking about her past. "Sophie married Assan Ang at nineteen years old in an arranged marriage in Thailand, her mother's doing, I understand. He held her captive in their apartment in Hong Kong until her escape to the United States to join the FBI. The Bureau had headhunted Sophie for her language abilities and tech talent through the computer college that she attended in Hong Kong."

"We are aware she claimed to have suffered abuse at the hands of the victim," Chang said.

"It was more than simple abuse. Sophie was not one to talk about it or draw attention to what she had been through. I think she spent a lot of time and energy trying to minimize the psychological damage Assan Ang had done to her. But I personally witnessed the violence against the first man she dated since her escape, inflicted during Ang's brutal attempt to kill him. Alika Wolcott barely survived. He was in the hospital for weeks, and ultimately went back to Kaua'i to try to rebuild himself and his business. I also witnessed what Ang did to Sophie after murdering a surveillance mole he'd planted in Security Solutions to monitor her. Sophie survived that confrontation and took him into custody, but he swore to kill her the first chance he got. Sophie called law enforcement anyway to deal with him, trusting us to make him pay and keep her safe. We failed to do that when Ang escaped from FBI custody during extradition to Hong Kong. Sophie knew she was on her own to survive, in spite of our best efforts."

Marcella described the FBI's investigation into Ang. "The man was connected to organized crime in Hong Kong and in the US, which is why he'd been so hard to capture. Honestly, it's a miracle Sophie survived and escaped, let alone did what needed to be done to that piece of filth."

Chang gave a humorless chuckle. "Please. Don't hide your real feelings about the victim and the crime."

"You called me in to make a statement. I am making a statement. Everything I have said has already been documented. Ang was a federal prisoner for his extensive drug and weapons smuggling, as well as murder and the attempted murder of an FBI agent."

"Were you aware that Assan Ang was unarmed at the time of his death? And that his throat was slit from behind? Hardly the usual self-defense scenario."

"Ang was holding our mutual friend, a decorated police sergeant, hostage. He was torturing her to gain Sophie's compliance. Ang didn't need to have a weapon on him to be deadly and to be leading Sophie to a death by torture and rape."

"But in the end, she was the one with a knife, wasn't she? And he was not."

Marcella bit her tongue on the stream of curses she wanted to let fly. The man was blind to the nuances, to his own bias against women, and to the big picture of the case! But screaming profanities was unlikely to change Chang's opinion. *Perhaps there was room on Assan's hell-sizzle frying pan for Chang, too.*

"I believe my client has made her statement and we've now begun circling the airport, so to speak. Do you have any more specific questions for her?" Lovett spoke up at last.

Chang hammered at Marcella for a while from different directions, asking his questions in different ways and posing speculative scenarios about why Sophie had dispatched Ang the way she had. Marcella did her best, sticking to her statements: that Sophie knew the victim's mindset, knew Ang had only harm planned for both Sophie and Lei Texeira, and had killed him to neutralize that threat and rescue her friend as expediently as possible. "If Sophie had wanted revenge, she could have taken it, maybe tied Ang to his sex torture wheel and cut off his relevant parts with her knife after a good flogging—and that still wouldn't have been enough to even the score, in my opinion," Marcella spat. *God forgives; Italians do not.* Marcella couldn't muster even a mental chuckle about that old saying. She couldn't imagine feeling any differently than she did right now toward Assan Ang. He'd gotten off light with a quick death.

"And yet the forensic evidence suggests that the victim was fleeing, and that she dispatched him brutally from behind with no warning at all," Chang said.

Marcella had had enough. She stood, straightened her blouse, and locked eyes with the DA. "I don't believe I have anything to add to this witch hunt. Good luck painting Assan Ang as a helpless victim."

Lovett stood, joining Marcella. "Let us know if you need anything further. The FBI always seeks to work cooperatively with local justice and law enforcement."

Marcella snorted. She pushed out of the office and the young man trotted to keep up as she headed down the hall.

Outside, she whirled to face him. "Thanks for all the support in there."

"You didn't need my help," Lovett said. "And well you know it."

That was true. *Maybe the guy did have a pair.* Marcella scowled. "I don't like the way he's trying to set Sophie up."

"I don't either," Lovett said, and Marcella felt a chill all the way to her bones.

CHAPTER ELEVEN

CONNOR'S GHOST program searched the internet for keywords related to District Attorney Alan Chang.

Chang had lived in Hawaii twenty years, emigrating from China under the sponsorship of his uncle, Terence Chang. He'd gone to university in Beijing but had done his JD at University of Washington and moved to Hawaii upon graduation, taking a position in the public defender's office and gradually working his way up the ranks. His immediate family consisted of Judy Wong Chang, a third-generation Chinese, and two sons aged ten and fourteen.

The man's shiny Teflon coating had to have some flaw. Connor surfed over to the DA's financials.

Nothing much of note; Chang's checking and savings reflected the middle-class salary of a civil servant at the lower end of the nationwide spectrum—such jobs in Hawaii often paid less. Perhaps it was assumed that a pretty setting made up for low pay.

Was Chang likely to go after Sophie on a murder charge?

The Ghost scrolled through the man's cases. A pattern of ambition shone through like a vein of fool's gold: the prosecutor went all in when he had something or someone headline-grabbing or controversial.

Chang was out to make a name for himself.

But perhaps he had done that, in achieving his spot as the DA? Connor doubted it. Chang probably had his eye on a judgeship.

But would prosecuting a female former FBI agent, a documented domestic violence victim, be the kind of publicity that Chang's career would benefit from?

Not likely, unless he had some other reason to go after Sophie—such as ties to Hong Kong, and the interests of Assan Ang.

Connor plugged a few more keywords into the search algorithm. As he waited for the network to assemble its findings, the Ghost stretched back in his chair, looking through the deeply tinted glass of his penthouse aerie overlooking Diamond Head and Waikiki. The glass was bulletproof and, even at night, opaque—but Connor's view of the ocean and the panorama of active cloudscape was unimpeded. He preferred this view to any art; there was always something to see on the arc of beach or in the lineup of surfers off the breakwater.

It had all worked out perfectly.

Except for losing Sophie. But he would win her back, in time. He had to believe that.

Beside him, Anubis sat up, inserting his silky head beneath Connor's hand for a pet. "Missed you, boy," Connor said. "One more thing I owe Sophie for." The Doberman was still moping for her and Ginger, her exuberant Lab.

Connor focused with an effort on his computer screen, willing his mind to engage with the streams of information tangled like visual threads on the monitor. He never used to have to make such an effort to focus. Sophie was still a big distraction—but not one he wanted to live without.

The Ghost's online search for connections bore fruit. *Chang had family connections in Hong Kong.*

As Connor researched the names of Alan Chang's relatives, they popped up as members of a well-known crime family with connections in Hong Kong, mainland China, and Hawaii. Terence Chang,

Alan's uncle, had died in prison on a racketeering charge, murdered by another inmate.

"You've got a few skeletons rattling in your closet, Mister District Attorney," Connor muttered.

Could the man's angling for a judgeship be more than personal ambition? What better way to help his criminal relatives than to be the district attorney, and later a judge? If Connor dug deep enough, he'd find the ways the DA was being influenced to help the Chang family. He just had to keep looking.

CHAPTER TWELVE

THE DARK in the cave was so thick it felt like its own substance. Was it Jell-O, sliding across his skin? Or was it oil, parting around him, filling his lungs every time he breathed?

Thinking about the dark added to Nakai's fear. "I am a blind man. And blind men get around just fine."

Nakai's voice echoed a little less. Maybe the lava tube was getting smaller; it was heading downhill, he knew that much from the direction of the stream, but would he be able to get out the same way the water was escaping? The water clearly changed height in this stream; hopefully it wouldn't flood while he was stuck down here.

One more worry. Don't think about it! Or turn it to something else. Like his thought about being blind. That had helped. He kept his eyes closed because blind men didn't need open eyes. The waves of panic at not being able to discern even a glimmer of light had receded. He didn't need to see to get around just fine.

He just had to keep moving and not give in to fear.

The fear felt like a monster, crouching with him in the dark, reaching out and tickling its claws across his skin, wrapping a freezing paw around his ankle.

He kicked his ankle, just to remind himself he could. A song came to him and he began to sing, remembering that the sound carried in the cave. If he sang, maybe someone would hear him. When he sang, the fear-monster drew further away. He didn't know many songs, but the one he liked the most was the Hawaii state song. Singing it, he remembered all the years he had stood with his classmates, hand over his heart, facing the Hawaii flag and the United States flag in the corner of his classroom. School had been a happy place.

The Hawaiian words flowed out, filling the darkness, chasing away the monster, making him forget his hunger and cold as he crawled slowly. He sang, until his throat was hoarse and he had to stop and drink more water. He rested a while, humming, and the humming was good, but not as good as the singing.

Maybe when he got out he would be a singer. He loved playing the ukulele, and he had an uncle who was a performer at one of the hotels. Uncle had taught him, and, sitting in the dark, Nakai held his hands as if he were playing the instrument, his fingers plucking as he hummed the simple song.

And when he had rested a while, plucking his imaginary ukulele, he felt calmer. No matter how long this took, he was going to get out. He was going to grow up, and be a famous musician. He would own a fine big home, and have his own family, and every evening he would light a fire because he didn't like the dark, and he would play the ukulele and sing.

Nakai dug a hole in the loose pebbles near the underground stream, wondering if he could get warmer. He folded himself into the hole and pulled armfuls of pebbles over himself. Even though the stones made him colder at first, after a while, they felt like a blanket settling over him.

A worm wriggled in Nakai's hand as pebbly sand sifted through his fingers. *He'd found something to eat during this last period of wakefulness.* Downing raw worms was gross, but he got through swallowing their slimy crunchiness by imagining he was a mongoose.

This mongoose, tough and determined, popped a worm into his mouth and chewed briefly, then swallowed it with a gulp of water. Mongooses ate anything and everything, and had no problem with worms or raw fish. If Nakai found a fish, he'd eat that raw, too.

Yes, he was just a blind mongoose, eating worms and curling up in a hole in the ground. He settled under the weight of pebbles over his body and curled up, almost comfortable in his snug hole.

He wondered if his mother missed him. Enola really didn't care about much of anything beyond her bong and her pipe these days, but she'd been a good mom when he was younger, fixing him breakfast and making sure his clothes were clean. It had all gone downhill when she'd hooked up with that meth-head jerk, Regal, and had listened to his lies about how the stuff would give her energy and make her able to work double shifts at her hotel job.

And when she lost her job, and their little rental, and Regal had dumped her, Enola had pulled Nakai out of school to live in Kalalau, "where we can breathe free air."

Nakai blew out a breath of the cool, musty "free air" he was surrounded with, fluffed his mongoose fur, and curled his long mongoose body tighter to stay warm until he fell asleep.

CHAPTER THIRTEEN

MARCELLA DROPPED her purse onto the small, plantation style hutch inside the door of the little cottage just outside of Honolulu that she shared with Marcus Kamuela. Marcus's mother had given the hutch to them as a housewarming present, telling her that these simple, screen-and-scrap-wood pie safes had been issued to sugarcane workers on the plantations back in the day. This particular one had belonged to Marcus's grandfather, and Marcella appreciated what a family treasure it was. She pulled out the drawer at the bottom, made from the wood of an old crate. The markings from the Hormel SPAM company on the wood were still bright from lack of sun exposure inside the drawer.

Marcus loved SPAM *musubi*, a surprisingly delicious concoction of fried meat and compacted white rice, all wrapped in a piece of dried seaweed. It was so popular that Anna Scatalina was now serving a variation with Italian sausage as one of the breakfast choices at the restaurant.

Marcella and Marcus had been living together for several months now, and just when she didn't think things could get better between them, they did. She felt guilty at her happiness whenever she thought of Sophie's many challenges.

Marcella greeted her betta fish in his bowl on top of the hutch. "Hey, Loverboy."

Loverboy had had several incarnations. This one was purple, with showy red tips to his fins, and he rammed the glass with his head at her tap. She sprinkled a few food pellets into the bowl. "Cool your jets. Mama's home."

Her fish fed, Marcella opened the small, heavy-duty gun case inside the hutch's drawer and stowed her weapons. In the bedroom, with its casual rattan furniture, she changed out of her sweaty work clothes and took a shower.

Marcus would be home soon, and she had a couple of phone calls to make.

The day had gone smoothly after the ugly deposition. The meatball subs, soggy or not, had been appreciated at the office, and after sharing them with Ken Yamada and Matt Rogers, she'd spent time down in the IT department with Sophie's young nemesis, Bateman.

That pink-cheeked, unassuming young man had surprising talent in his fingers and was helping her try to track Sophie online. They had looped into facial recognition at the airport to no avail, until Marcella remembered that Sophie would have Ginger. The large, friendly Lab was hard to miss. Scanning for Ginger in the footage, they had been able to spot the dog being shipped to Kaua'i.

Marcella took out the postcard, creased from being in her pocket. It appeared that she had found a clue. But why wouldn't Sophie just have texted her where she was going?

Because she didn't want to be stopped from going, and she didn't want to do time for killing Assan, no matter what the DA decided. Marcella understood that much.

But a lifetime of running? That was a good idea? Frustration with Sophie's choices rose up in a wave of heat. Marcella stomped across the dining area into the kitchen. She poured herself a glass of Chardonnay, picked up her phone, and headed to the little screened-in back porch.

They had been lucky enough to get an old plantation home on the

50

outskirts of Honolulu. Marcella loved having a yard, even though with their schedules they hardly had time to mow the scraggly grass. The huge mango tree, already dripping with fruit, shaded the porch against the late afternoon sun. Marcella sat on a rattan chair and scrolled through her contacts to the phone number she had extracted from Kendall Bix at Security Solutions. It was time to reach out to the Ghost.

She wasn't surprised when the phone rang to a mechanical voicemail and no one picked up, but that didn't help her frustration. She suspected it came across loud and clear as she left a terse message for Hamilton to call her back at this private number at his earliest convenience. Ending the call, she sipped the wine distractedly, staring unseeing at a pair of mynah birds hopping around in the long grass, looking for insects.

Sophie was on Kaua'i. And there was one person she knew well enough to call on Kaua'i. Maybe she was stirring the shit, but it was no more than her friend deserved after ditching Marcella and leaving her to clean up the mess.

Marcella scrolled to a number she hadn't called in a year. Her mood lifted immediately when the phone was picked up. "Hi, Alika. It's Marcella Scott on Oahu—got a minute to talk?"

CHAPTER FOURTEEN

"HEY MARCELLA. WHAT'S UP?" Alika didn't know why he'd picked up the call from Marcella. He remembered Sophie's bombshell Italian friend well—those two women sparring at Fight Club had brought the entire gym to a halt to watch them more than once.

"We've missed you over here. I was so sorry about how things went down, and that Marcus and I didn't get to say goodbye when you left. How's the recovery?"

"Fine. Great. Good as new." Alika glanced down at his body. He'd worked hard to recover from a near-fatal beating with a metal pipe close to a year ago. An ambush by professionals had left him with a broken leg, arm, and ribs, and a concussion that had put him in a coma. Rest, rehab, family support back on Kaua'i, and physical therapy followed by grueling workouts with a personal trainer specializing in injury recovery had eventually won back his strength —but Alika had lost interest in the MMA fighting scene that had been his focus for so long. He now preferred surfing and paddling his solo canoe. Time alone on the ocean brought him the most peace.

Alika squinted at the building he was working on, a triplex town-house in a planned "green" community outside of Kapa'a. The framing was going well, and his work crew was hard at it. Creating affordable, environmentally friendly housing while keeping his business healthy had gone a long way to distract him from the terrible events on Oahu.

"I'm happy to hear you're doing well." Marcella cleared her throat delicately. "I'm calling about Sophie."

Alika took off his hard hat and pushed a hand through his hair. A slight breeze from the north dried the sweat off his brow. He sighed, sorting through his response. "I'm sure Sophie told you we...said goodbye to each other."

"Yes, she did. And normally I'd respect that, and your choices, especially after all you've been through that can be laid at her ex's door. But she's in trouble, Alika, and I think she's on Kaua'i." Marcella proceeded to tell him the chilling tale of Sophie's struggles with her ex. "She finally got the better of him and killed him, but because of the way it went down, it's not a clear case of self-defense. The DA wants her to come in and be deposed, but...she's gone dark. No communication, no way to track her."

"I'm not sure what this has to do with me."

"I guess I need to spell it out. I know she went to Kaua'i, and I think she hiked to Kalalau. She's traveling under an assumed name, but she has Ginger with her. Can you take that helicopter of yours out there and look for her? Seriously, I wouldn't ask if I weren't really worried that this DA will get wind of her running and issue a warrant for her arrest."

Alika's heart rate spiked as he remembered Sophie. God, she was beautiful, with a face like Nefertiti and an unbelievable body: all long legs, lean muscle, sweet tender curves, and skin like caramel—and she was so much more than that. In the five years that they'd trained together, he'd come to know a woman smart enough to be a rocket scientist, brave, persistent, kind, and shy. Breaking up with Sophie was the hardest thing he'd ever done, but he hadn't wanted her to have to deal with his troubles with the Oahu mob and the long road to recovery he'd known was ahead.

"I don't know," Alika said. "I heard Sophie's with someone. I'm sure her boyfriend wouldn't want me involved." He had a lot of friends on Oahu who kept him informed.

"That guy...don't get me started! I don't want to bend your ear with all the backstory, but let's just say he's out of the picture permanently. I hope. Seriously, I wouldn't be asking if I had anywhere else to turn. I can't call any of my law enforcement contacts and twig them to the fact that she's on the run. This is a huge favor, pure and simple, and of course, we'll make sure you're reimbursed for any expenses. And if you don't find her...well, at least I'll sleep better knowing that we tried."

Alika straightened his tool belt, adjusting the hammer and measuring tape that hung at his waist as he paced back and forth, considering. Wouldn't he help a friend in trouble if he were asked? And Sophie was so much more than a friend.

"Okay." Alika's heart beat with heavy thuds as he agreed to this fool's errand. "I'll take my bird out. It's been a while since I flew the Na Pali Coast, and that's always a pretty run. Anything besides the dog I should look for?"

"I think she'll be trying to blend, but you know Sophie. She stands out in a crowd. You should also know that she's been through a lot since you left. She was shot. The injury scarred her face."

"I heard. I'm sorry about that." It had been painful not to reach out when Alika had heard Sophie had left the FBI and been hurt on one of her freelancer cases—but a clean break was what he'd chosen. He was trying to move on, especially once he'd heard she was dating again. He'd even put up a profile on a dating site recently, not that he'd done anything else with it. "I'll let you know if I find her."

"Thanks, Alika. I know this is outside the box. I owe you one." The agent ended the call.

Alika put his hard hat on and headed back onto the job site. Flying to Kalalau tomorrow in his Bell Jet Ranger would be a nice change of pace. He wished he really was as casual as he'd managed to sound, that his gut wasn't knotted with a combination of excitement and dread at the thought of seeing Sophie again.

He'd sure as hell never been able to forget her.

CHAPTER FIFTEEN

THE NEXT MORNING, Sophie put Ginger on her leash, strapped on her hiking boots, and headed back toward the main trail. She hadn't been able to find any opening leading to where the singing had been coming from. Intuition told her that the mysterious singer was the missing boy Enola had told her about. The woman had also said something about lost boys living in a cave. Maybe someone back at the camp knew more and her information could help find him.

The tent village was no longer deserted. A tall, tanned man with a heavy mane of wild hair and a sarong knotted at his hips approached her as she walked into the area. "Eh, whatchu doing back heah?"

"Hello. I'm camping over there." Sophie gestured. "I am here because I met a woman named Enola. She was looking for her son. She said he was with a group of boys who were all living together in a cave. Do you know anything about that?"

The man eyed her up and down taking her measure. "What's your name?"

"Sandy Mason. I just want to help. That woman seemed so distressed."

"Enola, she always get plenty *pilikia*." The man gestured with a muscular arm. "I'm Tiger. Come. You meet the camp. We don't just talk story about our business with any kine stranger who comes up this way."

Sophie followed the leader into the heart of the encampment, mindful of the watching eyes all around them. She smiled and Ginger gave a little woof of welcome as several children, wearing very little, came out of the tents and tree houses.

It was Ginger, not any of Sophie's awkward overtures, that got the two of them welcomed into a main covered area, where a fire pit vented smoke through a central rift in tarps overhead. Logs, placed around the fire pit, provided seating. Against one plastic wall, a woman stirred a pot of savory-smelling stew on a camp stove. "We about to eat," Tiger said. "You can stay. *E komo mai.*"

People trickled in from the other dwellings, everyone talking in a friendly way as the woman ladled stew into their bowls and they took seats around the fire pit.

"Do any of you have any idea where Enola's son might have gone?" Sophie asked, seating herself with a hand on Ginger's collar.

"Enola and her boy had plenty *pilikia* for long time," the woman stirring the stew said. "That sistah, she get one drug problem. The boy, he no like how she been acting. So he left, went live with the lost boys and the Shepherd."

"Enola knew that he was there. She told me that he disappeared from there; that's why she was so upset." Sophie received a plastic bowl of stew from the woman. She took a bite filled with vegetables, rice, beans, and taro, a purple tuber chopped into chunks. Flavored with a bit of rock salt, the stew was satisfying and looked quite healthy. "What is *pilikia?*"

"*Pilikia* is Hawaiian for trouble. Enola was not a good mom."

That wasn't a surprise. Sophie was pleased to see that the cook had also given Ginger a bowl of the same stew. The dog ate it with enthusiasm, tail wagging. Anything that didn't lighten Sophie's food supplies was a good thing.

"Who are these 'lost boys' and why are they living in a cave with…someone?" Sophie tried not to seem overly curious—the villagers were obviously cautious toward outsiders.

"We just call them that after Peter Pan," Tiger said. His smile was a brief flash of sharp, white teeth. "They are runaways from the island. The Shepherd is a wise man, a teacher. He takes care of them, makes a home for them in his cave."

"Even so, Enola seemed awfully concerned about her boy disappearing from the cave they live in when she met me at my camp," Sophie said. "She was going down to the beach to get help looking for him."

Everyone froze. Sophie looked up to find Tiger frowning. "How long ago was this?"

"Yesterday morning when I was setting up camp. I was disturbed, so I continued up this way."

"We no like da cops or DLNR come back heah," the woman in charge of the stew said. She had long thick gray-streaked hair in a braid and wore a muumuu that had seen better days. "We never get permits for live in the valley."

"I surmised as much. I too, am past my permitted stay." Sophie chased a last taro chunk around her bowl with her spoon. "Where do you go when authorities arrive?"

"We have our places," Tiger said evasively. "I take you to the Shepherd. We'll ask him about this missing boy." He took her bowl and picked up Ginger's. "We go. Everyone, you know what to do in case the rangers come."

CHAPTER SIXTEEN

THE BELL JET Ranger was a small craft designed for fast flight, maneuverability, and visibility. Alika rolled back the moveable plastic hangar behind his house in Kilauea where he stored the helicopter. Walking around the sleek aircraft with its bubbled Plexiglas windows, Alika went through his exterior pre-flight check.

His gut was grinding.

Why was he doing this? He didn't want to get involved with Sophie again. His leg, left arm, and ribs all ached at the mere thought, not to mention his heart. He'd fought hard to get his body and emotions back under control. *He was dangerous for her.* She was dangerous for him. The logic of a clean break made sense. This sketchy "rescue mission" did not.

But wouldn't he do something like this for a friend who was in trouble? If everything else was stripped away, Sophie at least had been that, and much more. His student for years in the MMA scene, Sophie had grace, power, and instinctive moves that had knocked him onto his back more than once. Alika had worked with her longer than she needed, truth be told, because he'd worried he'd lose contact with her once their coaching relationship was over.

She had been so damaged by that asshole ex of hers… It pissed him off that she'd rid the world of a monster and now might be facing a murder charge as a result.

That's why he was flying out to Kalalau. To help a friend. No other reason.

Plus, it'd been too long since he took out the Dragonfly. His private name for the helicopter described what flying it was like: sitting on the back of a powerful insect, and taking it wherever he wanted to go.

Alika had put together a backpack with overnight camping gear and food supplies. He tossed that into the narrow cargo area, strapping it down with webbing, and got into the cockpit. He radioed in his flight plan, got updates on the weather, and began the cockpit pre-flight check.

Firing up the Dragonfly gave him a burst of excitement he hadn't felt in months, and he tried not to think about why as he lifted the helicopter gently off the pad, turning to face the Na Pali Coast.

Rising airborne, he could survey his small kingdom. He continued a practice of living in one of the houses in his latest construction project until it sold. His current home was a Balinese teak beauty with a freeform pool and a lot of palm tree and bamboo plantings. The remaining homes in the planned green community were duplex townhouses, but they'd done a few eco-friendly luxury homes along the edge of the golf course, and his current abode was one of those.

Alika lifted the collective and directed the Dragonfly out to the coast.

There was nothing quite like Hanalei Bay, that great horseshoe of protected water fed by the thick artery of the Hanalei River and framed by a triptych of mountains. The layers of land, folded like green velvet curtains, were soothing on his eyes. He'd been working too hard lately, as he tended to do when left to his own devices.

Alika was back on his beloved Kaua'i, surrounded by friends and family, owner of a successful business that provided jobs and environmentally friendly, affordable homes. He'd rebuilt his body. He had no reason for the sapping depression that had been his companion since he left Oahu—but the truth was, he felt like a whipped dog, sent home and lucky to be alive.

These shitty thoughts weren't helping his mood.

Alika ducked the helicopter down, buzzing low over the reef at Tunnels surf break in Haena to see what the conditions were like. He spotted a whale, rising like a huge submarine under the water, spouting so close he could almost feel the spray, and that made him smile. The waves were too small for surfing, so a couple of standup paddlers were taking advantage of the conditions. As usual, Kaua'i's North Shore was stunning.

He probably won't be able to find Sophie, anyway. *This was a wild goose chase.* But still, his spirits lifted as the Dragonfly buzzed over empty beaches, calm rivers, and deep valleys, heading toward the rugged, spectacular series of red ochre and jungle-covered cliffs that marked the wilderness of the Na Pali Coast.

She was out there, somewhere, and he was going to find her.

CHAPTER SEVENTEEN

MARCELLA SIPPED HER WINE, staring out at the mango tree and thinking about Sheldon Hamilton. Was he really the Ghost? Could Sophie's wild accusation that he and Remarkian were the same person be true? It was so far-fetched, like something out of a freakin' spy novel.

But why would Sophie lie? Her friend really seemed to believe it, and the Ghost's betrayal had clearly hurt her, enough to push her right off the edge of her known world…

The front door banged, startling Marcella out of her reverie.

"Honey! I'm home!"

Detective Marcus Kamuela enjoyed shouting clichés like that. He also favored old TV shows like *Three's Company* and *Cheers*, classic cars, funky old houses, vintage Aloha shirts, and grand gestures— and she loved all that about him. She stood up, turning to embrace the big Hawaiian as he filled the doorway of the porch. "Oh good! I needed my daily hug."

"Is that all?" Marcus wrapped her close in burly arms, and then swept her into a dip as he kissed her, making her laugh and grab on for balance. "What's my favorite FBI agent doing out here on the porch, drinking by herself?"

"Grab a beer and I won't be alone." Marcella trailed after him as Marcus went into the kitchen and helped himself to a Longboard Lager. She refreshed her wine. "I have a situation."

"When do you not? Let's take a load off out back."

They settled themselves in the castoff rattan chairs that one of Marcus's sisters had given them for the cottage, and Marcella put her feet into his lap. "Foot rubs for sexual favors?"

"Who says foot rubs aren't already sexual favors?" He leered.

She laughed, enjoying the sight of his big brown hands kneading her foot, the bliss that traveled up her leg as tension ebbed. She watched him, her eyes only half open, loving the way the sun seemed to bathe his big body in warmth, catch in his black hair, and highlight the hard angles of his cheekbones and jaw. Marcus Kamuela was a hottie, no doubt about it, and he was all hers.

"So, tell me about this situation you've got." Marcus kneaded deep into her instep and she moaned.

"Cone of confidentiality?"

"Does it have to be a cone? Can't it be a cloak, or maybe even a cupboard?"

"You know where I get that."

"Yeah. *Get Smart.* And I love you for it." He lifted her foot and pressed a kiss to her ankle. "Spill."

"Well, there's this case that's been going on awhile that involves Sophie."

Marcus rolled his eyes. "Why am I not surprised? The only other friend of yours to be such a magnet for trouble is Lei."

"Well, that may be a little bit true—but they always solve their cases, right? And Sophie did exceptional work on this one, uncovering an online vigilante who calls himself the Ghost. She used her rogue DAVID software program to do it." Marcella took a sip of her wine, wondering how much to say, deciding the whole part about Sophie having an affair with the vigilante was not Marcus's business. "Anyway, the guy she was dating, Todd Remarkian—remember him? The Australian guy in charge of Security Solutions?"

"He got blown to shit in his apartment. Of course, I remember."

"Well, at his memorial she told me that Remarkian wasn't really dead. That the guy, Sheldon Hamilton, giving the speech at Remarkian's funeral, was the Ghost, and Remarkian's alter ego. Apparently, he's a master of disguise."

Marcus widened his eyes in comical surprise, dropping her feet and picking up his beer. "You gotta be shittin' me. This is like a James Bond movie."

"I know." Marcella sipped her wine morosely. "I believe Sophie, but I've got nothing on Hamilton, no way to prove any of the things she said."

"So whose ashes were at the funeral?"

"A man who looked a lot like Todd Remarkian but with close range blast damage. Hamilton had to have set it all up ahead of time. There was no DNA for Todd Remarkian to compare to the body, and DNA galore on file supporting Sheldon Hamilton's identity."

Marcus shook his head. "I get cases like a dude who bashed his neighbor on the head over a fence dispute and a couple of tweakers who kill each other for a hit."

"Well at least you get to close your cases. I just get frustrated and annoyed, chasing ghosts, as it were." Marcella dropped her head against the chair back and blew out a breath. "And to top it off, Sophie ran." This time, when Marcella brought her wine glass to her lips, it rattled against her teeth. Her eyes filled and stung. "Some friend she turned out to be."

Marcus set his beer down. "Let me take your mind off your troubles."

Marcella's heart rate picked up as he reached out to draw her onto his lap.

CHAPTER EIGHTEEN

THE CAVE WHERE THE "LOST BOYS" lived was a wide, deep opening beside a waterfall. Maidenhair fern trembled around the edges of the cascade, lacy against the shiny black rock of the cliff face. They'd come up an almost invisible trail branching off the main one; Sophie was sure she'd never have found the location without help.

Tiger picked up a conch shell resting on a rock beside the entrance and blew a blast, making her jump. "They don't like us just coming in," he said by way of explanation, and she nodded.

A few moments later, several young teen boys appeared. Lean and tan, they were mixed races and ages, dressed mostly in board shorts and ragged tees. To Sophie's surprise, they were armed, carrying a variety of clubs, a crossbow, and knives. Tiger they immediately recognized, however, and they lowered their weapons while keeping a wary eye on Sophie.

Ginger whined and strained at her leash to reach the tallest boy, who'd come forward. He had gray-green eyes in a deeply tanned face, and long hair snarled into dreadlocks, burnt blond at the ends from sea and sun. "Howzit, Tiger." The two did a brief backslap man-hug, and Tiger gestured to Sophie.

"This lady, she like help find Nakai. Enola wen' make humbug about her boy."

"Yeah, Nakai, he gone. He nevah like stay wit' us," Tall Boy said. "But no sense we look for him. He jus' gone, maybe back to Hanakapiai or all the way to Ke'e Beach."

"I'd like to speak to whoever is in charge about what Enola told me," Sophie said, polite but firm. "Is the Shepherd available?"

One greenish, three brown, and one blue gaze raked her up and down. "I told you. We no need help," Tall Boy said insolently.

"I was a security agent in the past, and I can find people. Enola came to me, and I want to help her locate her son." Sophie could feel their assessment of her clothing, her buzzed hair, her lean, taut muscles. "Take me to Shepherd, or I'll go in and find him myself."

"I like see you try," Tall Boy snorted.

Sophie reached out, grabbed the kid by the wrist, yanked him forward and flipped him. Tall Boy landed at her feet, gasping like a gaffed fish, and she rested her foot on his throat lightly as she looked around at the other boys. "Anyone else care to try me?"

No one else did. Tiger grinned. "You really were in security. You can help guard our camp when you're done here."

Sophie didn't respond, still waiting for the boys' response, and finally, a man stepped out of the shadowed doorway of the cave.

The Shepherd wore a long-sleeved tee that advertised Primo beer and a pair of baggy sweats with a *tapa* cloth *kihei* tied over the outfit at the shoulder. He had the rich brown skin of mixed Hawaiian heritage and a majestically white, full beard. Small brown eyes, set in dark pouches of ill health, tracked over her. "You come." He turned and led the way into the cave.

CHAPTER NINETEEN

N‍AKAI WOKE IN THE DARK.

"What you think, stupid boy?" he murmured aloud, echoing his mother's voice without the usual head-smack she so often gave. "You crazy. You wish you was dreamin' this whole thing." And yet, every time he woke up and opened his eyes, Nakai still had a long moment when he hoped this was all just a bad dream.

He was going to wake up one of these times in the tent he'd shared with his mother, the branches of the kukui nut trees overhead casting shadows on the fabric. Perhaps there would be something to look forward to that day: bodyboarding with friends at the beach, jumping off the cliff of a waterfall, maybe finding some ripe mangoes, or catching fish off the cliffs or prawns in the stream. Living off the land, he could always find something to both entertain and feed himself and others.

"But here I am, still in the dark, eating worms. I guess that's one way to live off the land." His voice sounded hoarse. *He was so freakin' unlucky.*

After twelve years of fending for himself with a druggie mom and no dad, he left her scene only to end up with a pedophile. Running away from that asswipe, he'd fallen through a hole into a lava tube labyrinth. Now he was dying a slow death from starvation, living on worms.

Worms. Their slimy texture, the way they twitched in his mouth, the flavor of blood and dirt... His belly rebelled at the mere thought of eating another one, and he retched.

Nakai uncovered himself from his latest hole, located the stream by feel, and began crawling in the direction of the water flow again. He was navigating faster now, and as long as he didn't think about it, the dark had become almost normal. So, he wouldn't think about it.

"I'm just a blind man, finding my tasty breakfast," he sang aloud, stopping to dig in the loose pebbles at the water's edge. *"Nobody likes me, everybody hates me, I think I'll eat some worms!* I can't believe there's a song about me. This is going to be a good story someday. Maybe they'll make a movie about how I survived. *Stayin' alive, stayin' alive, ah ha ha ha... Stayin' alive, eating worms!"* He sang a bit from the Bee Gees song. His mom loved that stuff before she got too tweaked out to notice much of anything.

The worms weren't that easy to find. Sometimes he dug for them a long time, maybe thirty or forty breaths. Breaths were how he'd begun to measure time. Every breath in and out was a time unit, and it made sense, because what else was there with any meaning down here?

Nakai lived on, one breath at a time—and by the time he finally found another worm, he was weak enough and hungry enough to eat it.

CHAPTER TWENTY

BREACHING the charred door of Todd "Connor" Remarkian's apartment in the ritzy Pendragon Arches apartment building the next day, Marcella wore rubber boots, gloves, a coverall, and a particle mask as she ducked through the crime scene tape. There was something to be said for good old-fashioned police work, because nothing told a story about what happened quite like a crime scene itself.

Until now she'd relied on data and information gathered by the fire investigators, bomb squad, and HPD to give her information about the "murder" of Todd Remarkian, but at this point, only she knew that the whole thing might have been staged. She really should have briefed Ben Waxman, her SAC, with Sophie's intel about Remarkian/Hamilton, but Marcella wanted to get a solid lead, some kind of intel or confirmation, before she told him such an outrageous story. Sophie had been Waxman's pet while in the FBI, but she was currently on the outs with the Bureau following a disagreement over the ownership of her rogue data-mining program, DAVID.

Nothing was ever simple where Sophie was concerned, least of all the situation with the Ghost. But if Sophie was telling the truth, this apartment had been the Ghost's home up until his staged "death" at the hands of Sophie's ex.

"What a tangled web we weave, when first we practice to deceive," Marcella quoted as she moved forward into the gutted apartment. Her partner, Matt Rogers, was back at the office working alone. She'd told him she needed to get her car serviced, and if the squint of his blue eyes was any indication, he hadn't believed her. He knew she was working on something involving Sophie. "And funny how one set of lies seems to spawn another. Thanks, Soph, for setting me up to lie to my partner."

That reminded her that Sophie's partner Jake Dunn had called again, frantic for word of her. "Did she text you? Anything? I know you know where her secret lair is!"

She'd brushed him off, too. "She's bailed on all of us, Jake. Her father's heard from her, so we know she's alive. That's all we have right now."

Marcella hadn't liked the pain that vibrated in the silence of Jake's non-reply. *The guy needed to get over her.* Sophie was seriously screwed up, first by what had happened with her ex, then the non-relationship with Alika, then the debacle with the Ghost—and now, she might be in big trouble with a possible murder charge. "I'll let you know if she contacts me, Jake, but I think we need to write her off at this point."

"Some friend you are," Jake had snarled, and ended the call.

If he only knew...

One more brick in the wall she'd have to take apart with her friend when she finally found her.

Marcella switched on her high-intensity light, shining it around the charred interior of the apartment. She breathed shallowly through her mouth, running the beam over the remains of furniture blown around the space and then moved aside by the investigation teams. Heavy soot streaked everything, and the air was close and reeked of smoke and fire suppression chemicals.

She wasn't sure what she was looking for. "I'll know it when I see it," she muttered to herself. "This guy was living a double life. Something in here has to show that."

She circled the space where the body had been discovered in the living area, marked in tape. Nothing of interest there. She moved through the open kitchen, feeling a twinge when she spotted a metal tin of the Thai tea Sophie favored resting on what remained of one of the cabinets. The metal sink had been dislodged and landed on the body, shearing off the toes—she'd never forget the sight of Sophie bending over that area, examining the corpse's foot with intense clinical detachment.

Marcella moved on to the bedroom. The door of this room had been closed and thus the damage minimal, confined to smoke and some charred streaking as the fire bled through the doorway.

A king size bed, draped in a classy but impersonal manly burgundy spread, gave no clue as to the identity of the man calling himself Todd Remarkian. The whole place was as generic as a hotel suite.

"And that in itself tells you something," Marcella said aloud, opening one of the side table drawers beside the bed to reveal a notepad and pen. Nothing else. "Don't you know that too anonymous is a clue, too, Mr. Ghost?"

Marcella went on to the closet, a walk-in affair lined in aromatic cedar that did little to combat the stench of the rest of the place. Her light moved across rows of shoes that revealed a casual but upscale style and racks of button-down shirts and neatly pressed chinos. Marcella felt a twinge. "These should go to someone who will use them. All these clothes need is a wash. But no. Not likely. Everything will just go into the landfill." She used a long shard of wood she'd picked up to poke at the shoe rack on the back wall—and she sucked in a breath of surprise when, with a protesting click, the wooden section moved.

"Holy crap." *The guy probably had a safe back here.*

Marcella wedged into the narrow space and wrapped her gloved fingers around the protruding edge of what looked to be a recessed opening. She pulled and pushed, jostling the shoes off the rack. Soot jammed the mechanism, but finally she got the rack open—and what she was facing was another door, this one without a handle but with a depression for sliding it aside.

She put her fingers in, and, grunting with effort, pushed the door open.

On the other side of the panel was a bedroom with an identical layout to the one she'd just come from.

"Holy crap," Marcella whispered again, and walked forward into the space.

CHAPTER TWENTY-ONE

SOPHIE LIFTED a hand in thanks to Tiger and followed the Shepherd into the dim of the cave, conscious of the teenage boys behind her. She tweaked Ginger's leash and brought the Lab close as she stumbled over a rock.

The cavern was huge inside, but the main light source after the opening was a fire burning deep within, venting up through some hidden space in the ceiling so that the air was fresh.

A living area had been set up near the fire, with a cooking hearth, rugs, and rolled-up pallets that she guessed were beds. Off to the right, barely visible, glowing from illumination within, was a large tent.

"Boys, go. We need to talk." The Shepherd gestured toward the tent. "My private area."

Sophie ignored the prickling of alarm at the back of her neck, and followed him.

Sophie paused at the door of the man's tent, lit dimly from the inside by an LED lantern's glow. She glanced back to see that the boys had withdrawn to the fire area.

She had nothing to fear from this old man; she could take him with her right hand tied behind her back.

The Shepherd gestured for her to enter, and she ducked through the zippered opening. A simple pallet with a sleeping bag was pushed against one wall. The LED lamp suspended from the center roof-rod of the tent cast a bluish light that hollowed their eyes and cheeks.

The man gestured to the pallet. "Please, have a seat."

"I have come at Enola's request. She is frantic to find her boy." Sophie settled cautiously on the mat.

"Yes. That woman." The Shepherd zipped the doorway shut, and Sophie reminded herself that the barrier was symbolic. There was no way he could trap her inside, or otherwise hamper her movements—she was strong, and armed with a good knife. The tent created a sense of privacy, but their voices would be audible to anyone close enough.

That knowledge shaped her thoughts as she said, "Apparently Nakai ran away from this group."

"Nakai was a foolish child." The Shepherd opened a folding camp stool and settled himself on it, leaning forward to rest his elbows on his knees. His dark eyes glittered with intelligence and a trace of malice. "The boy came to us, complaining of his mother and her drugs. And then, he didn't like the situation here, and he left."

"Did you see him go?"

The Shepherd shook his head. "It was dark. Bedtime. The boy was gone in the morning."

Sophie frowned. "Did any of the others see him leave?"

He shrugged. "I don't know. The boys do what they like." The Shepherd opened a small wooden box. "You like I should tell your fortune?"

This was unexpected.

Always find a way to get through to your interviewees by allowing them a sense of competency and control. Sophie's FBI training had provided needed instruction on engagement. Perhaps allowing this man to tell her fortune would build rapport. She nodded.

The Shepherd shook the wooden box. The container was almost engulfed by his large brown hand. A rattling sound from inside, and then he upended the box. A handful of bones tumbled out onto the gray nap of the tent's floor.

Sophie squinted at the yellowish objects in the dim light as the Shepherd reached up and unhooked the LED lamp, setting it down beside the scattering of bones. They were glossy and creamy-white with a patina of having been handled, and she was almost sure they were human. The Shepherd nudged them with a finger.

"I see a journey."

Sophie suppressed a smile. So cliché. *Of course, there had been a journey; she had to have traveled to reach a place like this.*

"Am I going to meet a tall, dark, handsome stranger?" Sophie and Marcella had gone to a fortune-teller at the Honolulu fair. The reading had been silly but amusing.

The Shepherd looked up. His eyes were opaque and so dark she could not see the pupils. *This man was no joke.*

"Three men. Two dark, one light." The longer he spoke to her, the more the Shepherd's pidgin slipped away.

What did that mean? Sophie schooled her face into the expressionless mask she had learned at her ex-husband's hands. "Go on."

The Shepherd looked back down at the bones and passed a hand over them without touching. She squinted, trying to guess the bones' age. *Not new, that was for sure.* She definitely saw a metacarpal and several phalanges.

"I see a resurrection after a death. I see a new beginning. I see a destiny that touches many, that could lead to destruction." The Shepherd looked up. "I see a reckoning at hand, and a fork in the road. Which way will you go? And with whom?"

A long moment passed. Sophie met the Shepherd's shuttered brown gaze, chilled by the accuracy of his insight into her situation.

He swept the bones into the wooden container and stowed it beside him. "An offering is customary when you've had your fortune told."

Sophie dug into one of her zippered cargo pockets and took out a twenty-dollar bill. The Shepherd slipped the money into the depths of his draperies.

"Did you see anything about the boy?"

"This was your reading. But I don't need to. He is dead."

Sophie stood, an abrupt uncoiling. Her head almost brushed the top of the tent. "How do you know this?"

"I have seen it."

"Did you kill him?" Sophie knew she'd overstepped before she'd finished the question. Damn her clumsy interviewing!

"It is time for you to go." The Shepherd picked up a small brass bell and rang it. A moment later one of the boys unzipped the door, Ginger thrust her head in, anxious. "I will rest now. Payton will guide you out."

Sophie pushed through the opening and followed the boy. Once away from the tent, she could breathe easier. She touched Payton's shoulder. "I would like to see the back of the cave. See if Nakai might have fallen somewhere."

She felt sure that the singing from underground was Nakai. Maybe there was some way he'd gotten lost from this cave.

The boy paused as if considering, then shrugged and led her deeper, toward a black rock wall in back. Sophie's hand dropped to the knife at her belt as she followed the boy and his light.

They finally reached the rough back wall. Sophie trailed her fingers along the rough lava as they walked for a while, but saw no further openings.

"Are there any other lava tubes nearby?" The subterranean "tubes" formed by rivers of lava traveling underground would explain how she could hear the boy singing, and how he could be alive and possibly traveling underground.

Payton shrugged. "We never found anything but this cave."

They had reached a small rockfall, and Sophie touched the boy to pause him. "Shine your light around those rocks."

The boy did. Scuff marks in the dust and sharp pebbles around the pile of rocks showed that someone had been back there, and a sharp reek of urine told a tale of body use. That did not mean anything except that someone had been in that area at some point.

"I have to go. Should not have brought you back here," the boy said abruptly.

"Wait!"

Instead the boy turned and jogged away with his light, the bouncing beam the only source of illumination.

Sophie stood still, letting her eyes adjust. She felt no fear in this situation; being left in the dark for extended periods had been Assan's favorite torture.

But without a light source there was no way to search further.

Still, she could surmise that there might be some entrance to an underground lava tube that Nakai had fallen into; if not here, then somewhere else in the area.

Sophie walked back to the entrance with Ginger at her side, passing through the boys' hostile stares. At the entrance, she heard the approaching thrum of a helicopter.

Could this chopper be the first responders that Enola had called for at the beach? Perhaps Sophie should meet them, take them to the place where she'd heard the singing in the rocks...

Still, she didn't want to draw attention to herself. Who knew if there was an APB out on her? Getting involved was a mistake. Approaching any first responders was a double mistake.

But only Sophie knew about the child's voice underground. She at least had to check out the helicopter. She pulled Ginger's leash and set off quickly down the trail toward its hum.

CHAPTER TWENTY-TWO

NAKAI DUG AND DUG. He could feel his fingernails tearing. He was weakening from lack of food, and he'd never carried extra weight on his wiry frame to begin with.

The worms seemed to have fled. Finally, feeling dizzy, Nakai tipped over and rested a while.

But resting wouldn't get him out of this place. *Resting would bury him here.*

After thirty breaths, Nakai got up and got moving again, crawling along, trailing a hand in the stream to rinse the dirt off and to reassure himself that he was headed in the right direction.

His other senses continued to help compensate for the lack of sight. The dark had begun to feel familiar enough that it no longer terrified him. The sense of being disembodied had abated; he definitely had a body, and though he couldn't see it, it never stopped talking to him, complaining of cold, bruises and wounds. His body was hungry and sore, and damn annoying.

As Nakai began to sing to keep himself company, he crashed into a barrier of fallen rock, banging his head and barking his knees. "Ow!"

He felt his way up, then down a rough wall of stone. He crawled from one side of the rockfall to the other, even tentatively feeling his way through the stream, which had found a way under or around the blockage somehow, backing up into a shallow pond in front of it.

"Damn it!" Nakai yelled, and slapped the water—and as if he had summoned a terrible djinn, the massive, invisible rock pile rumbled like a giant speaking in a language he couldn't understand. He splashed his way backward from the stones, scrambling away—but not fast enough.

CHAPTER TWENTY-THREE

ALIKA THROTTLED BACK the collective and settled the Dragonfly gently in a small clearing near the base of one of the waterfalls. Finding an opening that wasn't obstructed by branches and tree canopy was challenging.

This was his third landing spot since reaching Kalalau. He'd begun with the beach, that broad swath of yellow sand where the tourist boats landed regularly. Sophie wasn't there. He'd gone deeper into the valley, landing beside the stream at a popular camping area and showing a photo of Sophie and her dog that Marcella had texted to him.

No one had seen them.

Sophie had to be making efforts to stay hidden. Ginger was distinctive, and Alika glanced thoughtfully at the shadowed brim of a trucker hat concealing Sophie's face in the photo he could tell was ripped from a surveillance camera.

Marcella had said she'd been scarred by the gunshot wound she had taken on that case six months ago. There was nothing that could kill his attraction to her—but he wondered how bad the scar was, how she was living with such a challenge.

The rotors gradually settled, and Alika got out, locking the chopper. A happy bark of recognition brought up his gaze, and just like that, Sophie was walking toward him, Ginger straining at her leash.

Sophie's large brown eyes widened in shock as she recognized him. "Alika! What are you doing here?" She dug in her heels, bracing against the lab's enthusiastic tugging.

She wore unfamiliar clothes: a black tank top with a marijuana leaf striped in red-yellow-green Rasta colors, a pair of dark ripstop hiking pants and muddy boots. As the dog dragged her closer, he could see that Sophie's eyes were not even. When she turned her head to rebuke Ginger, the raised, pink outline of a skin graft arcing along her cheekbone and up into her hairline was visible, the skin slightly lighter than the rest of her face. Thinner than when he'd seen her last, Sophie was still gorgeous—only now that hint of tragedy that had always surrounded her seemed tattooed on her very skin.

"I came looking for you." No sense beating around the bush. This was no random encounter, and they had nothing to say to each other but the business Marcella had sent him on. "Marcella sent me. I'm here to take you back to Oahu for a deposition with the DA over there."

Sophie lost her hold on the leash, and Ginger hurled herself on Alika with all the enthusiasm of greeting a long-lost friend. He hadn't seen the dog in the weeks before he'd left Oahu when he had been recovering from his injuries, but the Lab clearly remembered him. He couldn't help laughing at her enthusiasm. "Down girl!" He caught Ginger's leash and handed it to Sophie as she approached.

Her unforgettable face had gone into that neutral expression he recognized from so many years of knowing her: an expression that hid her thoughts and feelings, a blank mask that shut him out. "Who did you say sent you? Marcella or Jake?"

"I don't know anyone named Jake. Marcella called and asked a pretty big favor." Some of his irritation at the disruption this trip had caused showed. "She led me to believe it was a crisis."

"I'm not about to leave for anything to do with Assan Ang. I'm in the middle of a different kind of crisis."

"Are you saying you didn't kill your ex?" Alika could feel his neck get hot at her determined tone, at the lack of warmth or appreciation for the hassle of this trip, and for his angst in having to see her again.

"I killed him, yes. But I won't go to jail for anything to do with him, no matter what the DA says." Sophie breathed hard, that indifferent mask slipping as her cheeks flushed, her dark eyes flashing. "He was going to torture and kill me. It was self-defense."

"Of course it was." Alika scowled, shook his head. "I know more than most what a monster you married."

Sophie cast her eyes down. Her lashes made shadows on her cheekbones. Damn...*that scar just made her look more dangerous and sexy*. Her long-fingered, golden-brown hand stroked Ginger's head. He glimpsed the Thai tattoos hidden on the insides of her arms. "I'm sorry. Again. For what Assan did to you." Her voice wavered. She lifted her eyes. "I will never say it enough."

"And it's not your fault. Assan hurt both of us. Thank you for killing him."

Their gazes met and held. He went still. *God, she was beautiful.* Inside and out, scarred and amazing and beautiful.

Ginger thrust her nose rudely into his crotch, breaking the spell. He pushed the dog's head aside with a laugh. "Hey, girl, mind your manners. This is a weird conversation, Sophie. Why don't you hop in the chopper and tell me all about killing that bastard ex of yours? We need to pick up more fuel in Kapa'a, but I can buzz you right back over to Oahu after that."

"No." Sophie shook her head, frowning. "There's a kid missing here. He's trapped underground, and I can't leave until I get him out."

Alika frowned. "Is this the crisis you were telling me you're involved in? What's going on?"

She told him a sketchy tale of a hysterical, drug-addled mom, the strange, cultish leader of a gang of runaways, a lava tube and a song heard through stones. "I think this boy's alive, trapped under those rocks where I heard the singing."

Alika glanced at the Dragonfly. "I can use my radio and call this in."

"Why don't you do that? But no, I can't leave until I show the first responders where I heard the singing. I'm going back to the rocks where I heard the voice, and I'm going to try to find a way to reach him. I don't want to draw attention to myself. And just so you know, out here, I'm Sandy Mason. And this is Gracie." Ginger wagged her tail, panting happily.

"You can tell me why you're traveling under an alias later, 'Sandy.' Hang on while I call the first responders. We'll see what we can get going for this kid."

Alika unlocked the Dragonfly and turned on the radio. He called in the request for help, all the while watching Sophie pace like a cat, her gaze searching the area as if watching for threats—or signs of the missing boy.

CHAPTER TWENTY-FOUR

Sophie could feel Alika's gaze burning a hole in her back as she forged down the trail ahead of him, heading back toward her camp. She'd let Ginger off her leash, and the dog trotted ahead, tail waving. No matter what bizarre occurrence was going on in her insane life, Ginger injected a note of normality and humor into every situation. Fixing her eyes on the dog's tail helped Sophie sort the riot of emotions she'd felt at the sight of Alika getting out of the helicopter.

Her former MMA coach was just as handsome and physically arresting as she remembered. His square, high-browed face broke into a surprised smile at the sight of her, golden brown eyes searching hers before he seemed to suddenly remember how they'd parted, shutting down, his full mouth thinning out and going cold.

Those shoulders! Alika must spend hours every day working out or paddling. He moved well, considering the shape he'd been in when she'd said goodbye to him after that near fatal beating, but walking toward her, she spotted a hitch in his stride that hadn't been there before.

Knowing that she was the one who had cost him so much still wrung her heart.

And now he had come all this way to fetch her, getting involved in her personal drama at Marcella's request.

Marcella must be angry at Sophie's departure with no word. "Pissed as hell, is more like it!" Marcella's voice supplied in Sophie's head. But right now, Sophie refused to think about the reason Marcella had gone to such lengths to track her down. She didn't have time for that—because the boy didn't.

Finding Nakai was what was important. The child couldn't last long down in the dark. Every time she imagined what he was going through, her gut tightened with her own memories.

Sophie pushed aside a wayward guava branch, then a sheaf of overgrown ferns, trying not to let them recoil and hit Alika. "It's not far, now." She should ask him about his life since the last time she saw him, perform some social niceties. Sophie struggled for words. "You look recovered from your injuries. Are you all right?"

"I get by. Not into the MMA scene anymore, though."

"Why not?"

"Don't know. I like solo sports now. Paddling my single man canoe. Surfing. Diving. Anything out in nature."

Alika's familiar voice, for years such a source of friendship and encouragement, still made her insides feel warm.

"Foul breath of a water buffalo," Sophie cursed under her breath. She wished she could call up Lei or Marcella and talk it over —figure out how to turn off those parts of her body and emotions that were responding to him...because she *was done with men. Forever.*

"What did you say?"

He must have heard her muttering. Sophie raised her voice but didn't turn, keeping her eyes on the jungle path. "Thank you for coming all this way. But I'm not sure I'll go back with you, even after we find the boy."

"Why not?" Alika sounded startled.

"I won't do time for Assan, no matter what."

"Until you go back, you won't know what the DA's thinking.

And if you keep running without even appearing for your deposition, they'll issue a warrant for sure." There was definitely a note of concern in Alika's voice.

Did he still care?

But this was not about that. This was about whether or not they could find Nakai.

Alika had called the first responders from his radio, and supposedly a search and rescue team were on their way. She wasn't even sure which agency had sent the team. "When you called for help, did they already know about the missing boy? Nakai?"

"No, they hadn't heard he was reported missing. I asked, because you told me the mother was the one who alerted you to his situation. But they had no other reports."

"That is odd. Enola seemed so determined to get help." Sophie kicked a large dried coconut out of the path. "We have to walk past a permanent encampment. I don't want to say anything about what we are doing. The people seem suspicious of outsiders." She glanced over her shoulder at Alika, and met his eyes. Her heart rate jumped. Even the way he'd ignored her overtures over the last year had not killed feelings based on the friendship and respect they had built up over so long a time in their coaching relationship, and that had formed during that brief time they'd been dating.

She still felt something for him. Damn it!

They reached the jungle encampment. The villagers, going about their business of fixing food, fire making, and other chores, looked at them but continued their activities with no outward hostility or withdrawal as Sophie and Alika continued on by.

Sophie was relieved not to have to interact. After their leader, Tiger, took her up to the cave where the "lost boys" lived, she had no idea what the people were saying or thinking about her.

Her tent remained undisturbed in its hidden spot.

"Good campsite choice. No one can see you from...anywhere." Alika grinned. His dimple was still adorable.

"The only reason you found me at all was that I came to you."

Sophie could hear how stiff and haughty she sounded, and cringed inwardly. "I heard the chopper and I went to see if it was a first responder for the boy."

"I'm well aware." His voice was dry. "I had already stopped in two places looking for you before I got to the waterfall area. I was about to leave after that."

Sophie tied Ginger to a sturdy guava tree near the campsite, filling the dog's lightweight travel bowl with water. The Lab drank thirstily as she looked up at Alika. "I know it cannot have been easy to come all this way and look for me. Break the silence between us. I understood after you ignored my texts. You don't want to be involved with me, so this must have been difficult."

"Sophie." Alika wrapped a big hand around her biceps and squeezed, a friendly gesture from their coaching days. "I wanted a clean break. It's what we both needed at the time. But I would never ignore a friend in need."

A friend. "You've been friend-zoned," Marcella said in Sophie's head.

Sophie made herself smile. "We understand each other, then. Thank you. Let's go find this boy."

Ginger gave a protesting yip at being left behind, tugging at her leash. She settled, looking guilty, when Sophie turned to scowl at her.

A smile tugged at Alika's mouth. "You've got your hands full with that one."

"She's got a mind of her own, as Americans say." Sophie pushed through a clump of ferns, headed for the outcrop of rocks where she'd heard the singing sounds. "But she's good company. Impossible to feel lonely with a dog like her."

"So...you've been lonely?"

Did she hear a hesitant note in his voice?

"Not really. I was with someone this last year. But it ended badly. Worse than us."

"I'm sorry to hear that." Alika's voice behind her was stiff and chilly.

Sophie concentrated on finding her way to the outcrop. "I'm unlucky in love. I've given up trying. Ginger and I are fine."

"And I haven't dated since I left Oahu. Too busy rebuilding my business and getting back my health."

"I'm sorry about that, Alika."

"Quit apologizing. Please. You killed that homicidal maniac and did us all a favor."

Sophie glanced back. Alika's gaze was hard and steady. "I hope the Honolulu District Attorney sees it that way." She looked ahead and spotted the stone outcrop. "Right over there!"

CHAPTER TWENTY-FIVE

MARCELLA SHONE the beam of her flashlight around the interior of a master bedroom that, this time, hinted at the personality of its owner. A vivid, slashing abstract painting filled one wall. A dog bed beside the king-sized bed told the tale of a canine pet.

Marcella put her hands on her hips. "The Ghost lived here, not there."

The stench of smoke and fire suppressant was still heavy, but when Marcella hit the lights, the power was on in this apartment. She flicked off her torch and walked through the bedroom into the hall.

Beside the bedroom was another door. She opened it and lifted the light switch, drawing a sharp breath. "Aha, Mr. Ghost. I've got you now."

With silver-gray walls and thick, sound-absorbingly dense carpet on the floor, the office was starkly utilitarian. One wall was lined with a long desk that held two workstations, each containing three monitors. A Bowflex machine took up another wall, along with a weight set, a pull-up bar, and a treadmill set at an extreme slant.

"So this is where you worked your magic, Connor-Todd-Sheldon-whoever-you-are. I can see you and Sophie here, clicking away on these monitors and hopping up and down for your infernal exercise breaks. You both are freaky."

Marcella took out her phone and called SAC Waxman. "Sir, I need you to come down here to the Pendragon Arches and look at something. I need help bringing in several computers. I have found where Todd Remarkian really lived and worked, for starters."

While Marcella waited for her boss and the FBI's crime scene backup, she prowled the second apartment looking for clues as to the occupant's whereabouts. She combed through the clothing in both bedrooms, the bureaus, and even the bathroom items. Everything was neat as a pin and nothing told her anything about where the man might be.

Still, if a harvest of DNA verifying the identity of the body was to be found, it was here. The corpse found in the other apartment had been identified as Todd Remarkian by dental records, and though the body had yielded DNA of course, there hadn't been a definitive sample to measure it against. This "secret" apartment had to have something they could use to rule out the body they'd cremated, and confirm that Remarkian wasn't really dead. And then she'd be one step closer to pinning the Ghost identity onto Sheldon Hamilton.

Marcella was sneezing convulsively from the fumes by the time the CSI team arrived, with Bateman, SAC Waxman, and Ken Yamada in tow. "I have to update you on a lead I've been pursuing," she said as the three agents took in the computer area, wide-eyed. "Agent Bateman, we need the hard drives off of these computers taken in, copied and analyzed. You can get on that while I show our SAC and Agent Yamada the rest of what's here." She sneezed again. "And I think we should talk out in the hall. I've had about all I can handle of this toxic atmosphere."

Bateman nodded, round blue eyes gleaming as he cracked his knuckles and set down a toolkit.

"I'm on it." The doughy young man was clearly impressed by a setup that would be catnip to any computer nerd.

She led the other agents through the bedroom into the hall and shut the door. "Whew, I hate breathing this air. Glad you guys brought along particle masks, at least. I'll keep this quick and we can talk more down at the station—but, operating on information I got from Sophie Ang, I found this mirror apartment." She briefly recapped what Sophie had shared at Todd Remarkian's memorial. "Sophie was angry enough at seeing Sheldon Hamilton there to finally break silence about his elaborate double/triple-life as the Ghost. She told me that Hamilton was actually Remarkian, and that the body discovered in the explosion was a cadaver he'd stored in case he needed to ditch that identity."

Ken Yamada's sharp brown eyes narrowed thoughtfully, even as Waxman's steel blue ones widened with anger. "Sophie withheld information on a criminal investigation!"

"Yes, she did. Because she was personally involved with the perp. And now she might be pinned with a murder rap while she's gallivanting off wherever she went." Marcella sneezed. "I'm glad you came, Ken, because you're the expert on the Ghost. We should work closely together on this and try to get some DNA out of this apartment and match it to Sheldon Hamilton." Marcella's phone rang. She pulled the device out of her pocket and glanced down, her eyes widening as she looked up to meet Waxman's gaze. "Speak of the devil. Sheldon Hamilton's calling me right now."

CHAPTER TWENTY-SIX

THE GHOST WAITED IMPATIENTLY as Scott's phone rang, watching the FBI agent through the video surveillance cam in the ceiling of Pendragon Arches. She finally answered. "This is Special Agent Marcella Scott."

Sophie's friend sounded out of breath. He could see why: she'd been fumbling to turn on a recording and tracking app on her phone before she took his call.

Ambivalent and guarded, Connor stroked the small goatee decorating his chin, pressing the adhesive down firmly as he watched SAC Waxman, whom he recognized from the Bureau's staff roster, follow her into the hall to eavesdrop. The two hunched over the phone just outside his former apartment.

"Agent Scott. This is Sheldon Hamilton returning your call," Connor said, adopting that identity's urbane manner.

The overhead cam distorted his view of Marcella. She was obscured by a particle mask, gloves, and booties, and she shucked the gear impatiently, hitting the speakerphone feature on her phone and holding it out toward Waxman. "Mr. Hamilton. Thanks for returning my call."

A tiny spinning skull in the corner of Connor's feed marked her phone's attempt to trace his call, but he was using computer voice transmission and had multiple VPNs masking his location, so he wasn't worried that she could locate him—and in addition, he was airborne.

He glanced out the window at brilliant midday clouds. "How can I help the FBI today?"

"I'd like you to come in for another interview to talk about Sophie Ang and your relationship with her."

"I told you already that I have no relationship with her. I thought we cleared that up in our last discussion, that rather rude interview after my partner's funeral."

"Listen, buster." Connor could hear the anger in Marcella's short breaths, see it in her rapid pacing. "We both know you did a number on Sophie."

"Buster? What is this, 1950?" Connor gave a relaxed chuckle. "I don't know what you're talking about."

Waxman waved at Marcella to pause, slow down, but clearly Connor had tripped Marcella's temper as the woman went on. "We found your secret lair, Sheldon/Todd whoever-you-are, and it's only a matter of time until we find your DNA in this apartment. I almost didn't believe Sophie when she told me that you had a double, even triple identity—but this place backs up her story. Things would be much easier for all of us if you'd just come in and tell us what the hell you're up to."

"I'm sure things would be simpler for you if I agreed to all your accusations. However, I'm on a business trip outside of the United States, and I have no intention of listening to any more of this nonsense. Further communication can be handled by my attorneys." Regret curdled Connor's belly. He'd wanted to joust with Marcella, play the game, watch her try to trap him and lure him in, but the woman's heavy-handed emotional outburst swamped him with guilt as he remembered how brokenhearted Sophie had been over his "death."

He was trapped in his own web of lies.

"Don't hang up! Sophie's in trouble!" Marcella burst out as his finger moved toward the disconnect button.

"I have no relationship with that woman. I've told you that repeatedly," Connor said, but his heart rate spiked.

"Sophie is off the grid, but she's scheduled for a deposition in the matter of Assan Ang's death. The DA seems to want to make a thing of this, and if you care at all about her... Maybe you can do something to help her. Warn her, at least."

Connor digested her words, his mind racing. He spoke deliberately. "Goodbye, Agent Scott. My attorney is the same one who works with Security Solutions. Any further communication with me can be routed through Bennie Fernandez and Associates."

Connor disconnected the call deliberately, proud of how cold his voice was. He really sounded like he didn't care two shits about Sophie.

Marcella stomped her foot and whirled to talk to Waxman. Much waving of hands ensued. The agent was clearly upset, and not for the first time, Connor wished the Pendragon Arches had invested in audio for their surveillance system.

Marcella looked frustrated now, but she was going to be even more so—because, before he set off the bomb that blew up "Todd," Connor had paid for a mob-connected cleaning service to go through both Pendragon Arches apartments and remove all personal trace.

He'd taken care of scrambling the computers he'd abandoned in the "Batcave" himself. That puppy Bateman, so diligently unscrewing the hard drives in the office, would find exactly nothing.

Connor was done playing footsie with the FBI. He had bad guys to turn against each other, justice scales to right. Outside of the United States was an even more target-rich zone than inside.

But Marcella was right. Maybe there was some way he could help Sophie from afar. She deserved at least that much from him.

The Ghost opened his tablet and went to work.

CHAPTER TWENTY-SEVEN

SOPHIE PICKED UP A SMALL, round rock and tapped on the largest of the cluster of boulders marking the place where she had heard that eerie rendering of the Hawaii state song. Just thinking about it made the hairs on her arms rise. If that was Nakai singing, the boy had an incredible voice. "I heard the sound carrying up through these rocks. I already looked around, and couldn't see any openings. But I feel confident that a lava tube below is how the sound came up so clearly."

"Did you try to signal him at the time?" Alika probed the ground around the boulders with a sturdy stick.

"I did not. To tell the truth, I was a little...haunted, I guess you could say, by the voice and its apparent lack of source. I didn't put it together with the missing boy right away." Sophie tapped the rock on the boulder in sets of three, the international signal for distress. Hopefully the boy would hear the rhythmic tapping and somehow signal them from below.

Alika continued to probe and push at the boulders. "I think we should go back and bring the first responders to this site. I wish my radio was portable so I could keep in touch with them from here, but

I have to return to the landing area to check if they've located my chopper."

"I understand. Too bad there's no cell service." Sophie grasped one of the smaller boulders and rocked it with all of her body weight. She was surprised to feel it give, moving with a grinding sound. "Help me! Maybe we can tip this one over and get a little closer to the top of the lava tube."

"I'm on it." Alika dropped his stick and grasped the stone beside her. Their arms overlapped, their bodies crashing into each other as they strained to tip the boulder over. "We need to coordinate our movements. On the count of three. Let's do this!"

Sophie wedged herself beneath Alika's big frame and grasped the rock with a new grip, rocking back and forth with him as he counted to three, and then heaving with her legs at the same time as he did.

She felt the power of their joint effort surge through both of them. The rock moved, giving an inch with a grind of protest, shifting within its earthen cradle. Sophie lost her balance and stumbled to her knees beneath Alika.

He grabbed her hand and hefted her back up, and his grin was infectious. "I forgot how great it is to work hard with a strong woman."

Sophie's whole body lit up at the compliment. Alika had never been intimidated by her or treated her like her strength was emasculating. She blew a breath past the tightness in her chest. "I think we need a few more of the same kind of moves."

They repositioned in a deep squat, side by side, arms crossed over the rock, and Alika counted. Again, with the heave, and this time Sophie didn't fall. Three more massive pushes, and the boulder tipped over reluctantly.

Panting, Sophie rushed around to examine the crater. "Looks like lava rubble at the bottom." They both dropped to their knees and dug at the hole in sync, shoveling rock, cinder, and dirt aside.

Twenty minutes of that and a hole appeared at the bottom. More scrabbling, and the hole widened.

"We are lucky the top of the lava tube's structure is thin here," Alika said. "Otherwise we would have needed a jackhammer and God knows how long to get inside. Looks like your guess was correct. I just hope the boy hasn't expired already."

Sophie couldn't take the suspense a moment longer. She leaned forward, bracing herself as she looked into the bottom of the hole. She called down into a blackness that seemed to rise up from it.

"Nakai? Nakai? Are you there?"

And then the lip of the hole caved in, and Sophie tumbled forward into space.

CHAPTER TWENTY-EIGHT

THE DROP WAS short and hard. Sophie tried to take the landing on her shoulder, but she felt the impact jar through her body as clods of earth rained down on her. As she hit bottom, her mouth filled with dirt. Instinctively she curled her arms over her head, pushing the dirt out of her mouth with her tongue, making a space for air with her arms in front of her face. Chunks and clumps of earth continued to pelt down on her, and she waited, breath held, for an endless moment to find out if she had been buried alive.

The stream of pebbles and dirt slowed. Sophie curled inward and lifted herself, rolling up onto her knees and throwing the debris off. She struggled up out of the soil and looked up into the light, wiping dirt from her face and eyes.

"Sophie!" Alika yelled. "Sophie, you okay?"

"I'm okay." She dusted dirt off of her arms and lowered her head to shake the earth out of her hair. Her shoulder felt wrenched, but when she rolled it back she could move it. She peered up at his backlit form. "How far down am I?"

"Not bad. About eight feet. I'll need to get a rope to pull you out —and this edge is still crumbling. I'll have to find a spot that can take your weight. Hang on while I look around."

"Okay." Sophie dug herself out of the pile of soil and stones, grateful that none of the heavier boulders had decided to follow her into the pit. She stood, her shoulder throbbing, knees shaky, and head swimming. She looked around.

Sophie was standing in an almost perfectly circular two-foot circle of blazing sunlight. Total darkness surrounded her in every direction.

Hopefully, the noise they had made would have alerted Nakai to their entry into the lava tube.

She stepped cautiously out of the light and into the lava tube, allowing her eyes to adjust. Cool air drafted over her, carrying the trickling sound of water. Reflected light from overhead gave a small area of illumination. She spotted a shallow hole dug at the edge of the stream.

That hole had been made by a human, and not long ago. She could see scuff marks in the pebbles surrounding it.

"I found a boulder I can attach the rope to," Alika called down to her. "Hey, where did you go?"

"Right here." Sophie stepped back into the circle of light to look up at him. The contrast was blinding. "There's evidence that someone was here recently. The boy is down here, I just know it."

"Great. That's one good thing to come out of this mess. I'm heading back to the chopper to get my rope and check on those first responders." Alika's warm tone told her how relieved he was that she was unhurt. "Don't move. I'll be back shortly."

"I'll be waiting."

He nodded, and disappeared.

Sophie sat down on the pile of fallen rubble, trying vainly to see into the gloom. If only she had her flashlight... She surrounded her mouth with her hands and called out into the tunnel. "Nakai! Nakai, are you there?"

A long moment passed, and then she heard a faint sound. Not a call exactly, more like a distant cry. She crawled down off of the dirt pile and walked forward into the dark. *Nakai was alive, and he needed her.*

"Nakai! I'm here to help you! Come toward this sound!"

She heard it again, just a tease of a whisper, just enough to identify a voice, and then a tapping sound.

Three taps. And then, three more.

An SOS.

Alika would be back shortly with the first responders to get them out. Thanks to Assan, she was comfortable in the dark. With a glance back at the column of light, so bright it seemed like a solid, Sophie rose to her feet and walked forward into the darkness.

She located the stream to one side of her and navigated by feel, her arms outstretched, her eyes straining involuntarily. She banged her shin on a rock and let out a yelp.

"Help!" Now she could hear a faint voice for sure. "Help me!"

"Nakai!" Sophie shut her eyes. She used to do that when Assan locked her into that hated windowless "safe room" that had been the site of so many of his tortures. Keeping her eyes shut seemed to reduce the exhaustion caused by a sense straining for information that wasn't available. "Nakai, my name is Sandy, and I'm here to help get you out."

She had lost the stream and its guidance toward the boy. Somehow, she'd wandered into one of the walls. It rose before her, jagged, poky with lava protrusions, and impenetrable. "I'm on my way."

"I'm trapped. Rocks fell on my leg," the boy yelled.

His voice echoed now, so close that he might as well be beside her. *Interesting effects happened down here with sound.* The irrelevant observation kept fear at bay as she felt down the wall, straining to hear the sound of the stream. What if the lava tube branched, and she went the wrong way? The tunnel must have curved away to the right...

"Are you hurt?" Sophie called back.

"Yes." She heard the break in his voice, the barely restrained tears. Adrenaline surged through Sophie and she dropped to a squat, feeling her way along the ground, navigating carefully over rocks and obstacles, heading toward the sound of water again.

Sophie sighed with relief once she felt the water on her hands again. She was sure Nakai had been following the stream—it made sense to stay close to it and hope it would lead to an exit. Afraid to lose the water again, she dropped to her hands and knees and crawled through the dark toward the boy.

CHAPTER TWENTY-NINE

NAKAI RAISED HIS HEAD, straining his ears to listen. He heard the soft crunches and shuffling sounds of the woman's approach. What had she said her name was? Sandy? *Why didn't she have a light?*

Not long ago, he'd woken from uneasy drowsing to hear a rumbling similar to when the rockfall had caught him. He'd cringed, wrapping his arms over his head.

In the many breath cycles since he'd been trapped by a boulder landing on his leg, Nakai had begun to hallucinate. Memories and images swept over him and played out in front of his eyes so vividly he was almost sure they were real. He'd just imagined one of his happiest birthdays so intensely it felt real: playing Super Mario Kart with his cousins, surrounded by the smell of pizza and the demolished remains of birthday cake.

Pain pulsed through him with his heartbeat, radiating from his trapped leg. Why couldn't he just die and get this over with? But alas, wishing didn't make it so. And if the woman was coming, maybe he would be rescued after all.

"Sound carries through the stone," he remembered Shepherd saying. He picked up the largest fallen stone he could and banged it down on another stone in sets of three. *Bam bam bam!*

"Oh, please let them find me, God," he whispered. "Please."

It seemed like forever, and he thought he knew where she was, but he still cringed and yelped when a warm hand touched his shoulder. "Nakai. It's me, Sandy."

"How do you know my name?"

"Your mother Enola came through my camp looking for you. She was so distraught that I had to try to find you." The woman's hands patted and brushed over him. She was trying to see how hurt he was.

"I am all right. Except for my leg. It's...buried." Bile burned Nakai's throat as a fresh wave of pain surged up his leg when Sandy jostled the rock trapping him. "Please don't touch it. I'm going to puke."

"Oh, I'm so sorry." Sandy had a soft rich voice with a little bit of an accent. Her hand brushed his hair softly. "Just relax. Help is on the way. My friend went to get a rope and he'll be coming soon."

His mother had tried to get help for him?

In all of Nakai's imaginings, that was not something he had even dreamed of. The knife of betrayal had slid between his ribs a final time when the fish he'd worked so hard to catch for them to eat was gone from their camp, traded to fill her crack pipe. He remembered his last words to Enola vividly. "You're a worse mom than a dog!" he'd railed. "At least a dog tries to feed its pups!"

He'd taken his meager possessions and headed for the cave by the waterfall, where he'd heard other runaways lived with a man who took care of them.

And look how that had turned out.

He was so unlucky.

Sandy's soft touch on Nakai's hair penetrated dark purple thoughts tinged with the red of pain. *He'd begun to see his thoughts in color, too.* Being down here was doing strange things to his mind.

"Hang on, Nakai. Just rest. You're not alone." Sandy's breath was sweet on the curve of his ear. *Maybe that luck was changing.*

CHAPTER THIRTY

IN THE FOUL-SMELLING hallway of Pendragon Arches, Marcella slid her phone into her pocket, done with her diatribe about the Ghost.

"You need a break," SAC Waxman's pale eyes were steely. "Go home. Take a shower. Get your emotions under control. You flubbed that telephone interview with Hamilton and scared him off."

Marcella scowled. "I thought I'd lay out my cards and tell him how close we were to nailing him."

"And that went well?"

Marcella cast her gaze down at her discarded protective clothing. She couldn't resist giving the filthy bundle a kick. "That man's a lying rat bastard!"

"As are most of our perps."

"But he broke Sophie's heart." Marcella reached down and picked up the clothing.

"For which neither of us will ever forgive him." The tone of Waxman's voice brought her gaze up to meet his. The look in his eyes made her glance away quickly. Waxman was not an enemy she ever wanted to have, and the Ghost had roused her boss's icy ire. Not for the first time, Marcella wondered about the nature of Waxman's attachment to Sophie.

"Well, you're right. I flubbed that. But at least I found his lair, and I'm sure the CSI team and Bateman will come up with something we can use to nail him."

"I hope you're right, but I'm not holding my breath. He's been two steps ahead from the beginning. Go home, Agent Scott. And we'll see you in the morning for a team meeting on how to move against the Ghost cyber vigilante."

"Aye, aye, sir." Marcella couldn't resist a sassy bit of attitude as she turned and headed down the hall. "And in the meantime, I'll be making a voodoo doll of this guy."

"Might be the only way we can reach him," Waxman said drily. Marcella's mouth tightened as she got on the elevator.

*If only she could get a hold of Sophie...*hopefully Alika was having some luck. Spurred by the need to check on that, Sophie called Alika's cell phone. It went immediately to voicemail, and she left a message asking for an update.

What else could she do?

She stomped her foot with frustration.

It was definitely time to go to the beach.

MARCELLA BEGAN SHEDDING her clothing at the door as soon as she reached home, kicking off her shoes, ripping off her shirt, flinging off her bra. She tore off her slacks and panties and tossed them in the hamper. Barely stopping to greet Loverboy in his bowl, she tugged on a bathing suit and grabbed a beach towel and her inflatable floaty mat. She poured some Chardonnay into a metal travel cup with the straw attached, and soon she was on her way to Waikiki.

Hawaiian local Marcus was a very good surfer, but Marcella was a Jersey girl who had not grown up spending time in the ocean. Bobbing peacefully on her inflatable while sipping a glass of wine was the best way for her to enjoy the water.

Soon she was doing just that, after a brisk swim to wash the stench of the burned apartment and the aftermath of frustration off of her body.

She loved coming to Waikiki in the evening. She could watch the tourists, the Japanese weddings, the surfers, and the Tai Chi class on the beach, all from the comfort of her lounger. She enjoyed a satisfying knowledge that, while many of these people had to leave, she could come here any evening she chose.

Lying on her float, looking up at poufy clouds tinted salmon-pink with evening as she bobbed in the sheltered man-made cove in front of the Hyatt Regency, Marcella enjoyed the gentle, soothing rocking of the ocean, its briny scent clearing the last of the smoke and chemicals from her nostrils. She finally closed her eyes on the beautiful scene of Diamond Head wreathed in sunset clouds, and just relaxed.

Her mind mulled over the events of the day. Dr. Wilson, a psychologist friend, had once told her that the secret to being able to think about her cases without getting stressed was to simply observe her thoughts, let them flow by, and let whatever insights or ideas that needed to, come to her of their own volition.

Sophie. Her friend's beautiful face appeared in Marcella's mind.

Marcella was trying to do right by Sophie, but she was still angry with her too. And as she observed herself, Marcella suddenly knew why Sophie had not told her about her involvement with the Ghost.

Marcella was first a cop, then a friend.

And she always would be.

Sophie knew that, and she would not have wanted to compromise Marcella's integrity or put her in a position to have to choose the friendship over a case. In that way, Sophie was being a better friend than Marcella was, harboring all this anger while outwardly "doing the right thing" to try to help.

Sophie had suffered enough, and would continue to suffer, because of her choices in men. *A real friend wouldn't hold that struggle against her.*

Marcella released a long sigh. In the end, Sophie had told her all she could about the Ghost, and she was no longer with him. All

Marcella needed to do now was release her anger and frustration. All that judginess. *Just let it go.*

She reached up to touch the slim gold cross her mother had given her at first communion in Jersey so many years ago. Though not a practicing Catholic, Marcella knew when prayers were in order.

"Dear God, please help Sophie find her way through this. Keep her safe. And bring her back, so we can be friends again."

Marcella felt a subtle release of emotion: a new compassion for Sophie, followed by a wave of gratitude. Marcella had it all: a secure job, a wonderful man who loved her, caring (if smothering) parents, good friends, her health, and good looks. What did Sophie have?

So little, right now.

Marcella heard an excited burst of Japanese from the tourist family on the beach nearby, and lifted her head off the inflatable pillow to look up at what they were exclaiming over as they pointed out to sea.

A rainbow arched down from one of the sunset clouds over Diamond Head, an extravagant statement of hope. The scene was postcard-worthy.

"I hear you, God." Marcella closed her eyes, and just let it all go.

CHAPTER THIRTY-ONE

ALIKA RAN down the jungle trail, headed back to the chopper. Urgency gave power to his stride as he barreled along, bypassing Sophie's hidden tent and the encampment village. He finally reached the main trail and turned up the path leading toward the waterfall landing area where he had first encountered Sophie. The track was wide enough to run, and jogging up the narrow, overgrown, boulder-studded trail reminded him of the hikes he and Sophie had enjoyed all over Oahu. Oahu had many good hiking trails, but the Na Pali Coast was so much less trafficked, and so spectacular.

He mentally pushed away the good memories—he had struggled to get Sophie out of his mind as he did physical therapy and tried to rebuild to where he'd been before... But it had been difficult, and now he was with her again. Her powerful body flexing beneath his as they tried to move the boulder had been sexy as hell, and also a great feeling of teamwork. Then, a few minutes later when she disappeared in a fall of debris, he'd about had a heart attack. *She was wrecking him all over again!*

The Dragonfly was undisturbed, and he unlocked the cockpit and activated the radio. Reconnecting with the first responder team he had notified on his first call, he added that his colleague had found evidence of the missing boy's existence in a collapsed lava tube, and that his partner had also fallen in.

"We have a fire and rescue team scrambling to get out your way in a chopper," the operator told him. "Sorry it's been so long already. They should be to your location in about an hour."

"I'll leave my chopper's transponder on so you can find me easily and park in this clearing. I'm going back to monitor the situation at the site. I will bring a walkie-talkie and leave another one on the outside of my bird near the door. The team should be able to reach me on the frequency I leave it tuned to, and when they contact me I'll guide them to the rescue area."

"Copy that. No cell signal out there, so that should work. Will advise the team to look for the walkie unit."

"Roger." Alika returned the radio to its cradle and turned off the unit. He reached into the netted storage area in the tail of the Dragonfly and took out an emergency survival kit containing a flashlight and pack of glow sticks, and a large hank of strong poly fiber rope. Looking around inside the chopper, he grabbed several protein bars and the first aid kit. No telling what shape this kid would be in. He transferred the items into a small day pack.

He locked the chopper up and slipped his arms into the straps. A zing of familiar pain shot up his ribs and down the arm that had been broken. His healed leg was setting up a steady throb, too, irritated by the strenuous uphill run.

"Nerve damage," his surgeon had said, when, months after the broken bones had healed, he still experienced strange, lightning-like bolts of sensation, as if the injured areas were all communicating in protest. "It should improve with time."

But Alika had learned to ignore the pain. It served no purpose. The pain did not mean that his injuries were getting worse, only that they had been there—like shadows cast by the beating, his body reminded him of it.

Alika headed back down the trail, this time pacing himself. The emergency team would be here in an hour. *Sophie was fine where she was, and whatever had happened to the boy, one hour more or less would not make a difference.*

Still, Alika was winded when he arrived at the boulders, the extra weight of the pack and his efforts catching up to him. He took a moment to chug a water bottle before going to the boulder he'd identified as secure and anchoring the rope to it.

"Sandy!" He called down into the hole. "I'm back with the rope."

Some part of him was not even surprised that there was no answer, and when he flicked on the powerful flashlight he had brought, shining it around in the hole as best he could, she was nowhere to be seen in the area.

If Sophie had heard that boy calling for help, she would not have waited for Alika's return, light or no light. She was comfortable in darkness, though he didn't know why. The dark of that lava tube was not the terror for her that it would be for most.

"Sandy!" he called one more time. No reply. "Damn it."

The first responders would be here in an hour; he was sure he could catch up with Sophie and help her before they arrived.

He tied knots every foot or so in the length of rope closest to where he had attached it to the rock. He checked the rope around the boulder with several yanks, leaning back with his body weight to make sure that it would hold him.

Alika tightened the straps of the supply pack and swung out into the hole, gripping the rope tightly at the knots and lowering himself into the cave.

At the bottom, he turned around, facing blackness in all directions. Truth was, he had no idea which direction she had gone, and the impenetrable black was disorienting.

"Sandy!" Alika curled his hands around his mouth. The shout was good and loud. "Sandy, tell me where you are!"

"This way!"

Her voice was faint but clear, and that was all he needed to head in her direction. Alika switched on the powerful flashlight and, cracking a couple of glow sticks from the survival kit, dropped them as he walked toward where he'd heard her call.

Shining the flashlight's beam around the lava tube as he went, he took inventory of a roughly eight- to ten-foot-high circular tunnel with a small stream of water to the left and jagged interior walls. The ground underfoot was lightweight, sharp *a'a* lava in frothing, bizarre formations. Smoother, waterworn stones and pebbles near the trickling stream provided an easier surface to traverse.

Drag and scuff marks in the edge of the stream showed that someone had crawled beside the water, and periodically, holes had been dug.

What was that about?

Alika pushed on, the flashlight bouncing—and suddenly he caught Sophie in the flashlight beam, kneeling beside a rockfall that completely blocked the tunnel.

A young teen lay flat on his belly beside her sheltering body. He looked up. The flashlight caught the boy's wide, unfocused eyes, and he screamed.

CHAPTER THIRTY-TWO

ALIKA KNELT ALONGSIDE THE BOY, keeping the beam turned away so that the light didn't hurt the kid's sensitive eyes again.

"Nakai, this is Alika. He's my friend, and here to help," Sophie said.

The boy nodded, a jerky movement. Clearly, every motion caused pain.

"Where are you hurt?" Alika touched the boy's shoulder gently.

"His leg is trapped in the rockfall. We are going to have to move the stones off of his leg to get him out," Sophie said.

Alika shined his flashlight carefully over the boy's body as Nakai hid his head beneath his arms, hiding from the light. The boy wore a filthy tee shirt and board shorts. He was covered with scratches and bruises, most of which were minor. His leg was, indeed, trapped beneath not one but several boulders. Setting the flashlight aside, Alika pressed his shoulder against one of the rocks, checking its weight, and just that slight movement made Nakai scream again.

He moved back and squatted beside the child. "We have to wait for the first responders to get you out. You'll need to be carried, and it's going to hurt. I have some supplies in my backpack. You are going to need your strength." Alika opened the pack, extracting the first aid kit, some more glow sticks, protein bars, and a couple of water bottles. "I have to go back and meet the rescue team to show them your location."

Sophie's eyes were large and haunted as she glanced up at him. She was clearly affected by the boy's suffering. "I agree we shouldn't try to move him ourselves. I'll stay with him."

"Good." Alika unwrapped a protein bar and handed it to the boy. "Nakai, don't eat too fast. Your body isn't used to it. But a few bites, chewed up well, might help you get a little energy for what's ahead. It's not going to be easy to get you out of here and back to get medical attention. We'll have to take a helicopter ride."

The boy spoke for the first time. "A helicopter ride!" His trauma seemed momentarily forgotten. "I've never been on one!"

"And you're going to love it. But it might be a little rough with that leg, so anything you can do to get stronger before the rescue team gets here will help the transport. Is there anything I can do for you, first aid-wise?"

"I'm okay, except for my leg," Nakai said. He took a bite of the bar and chewed, closing his eyes in bliss. "This tastes so good compared to worms."

Alika felt his eyes widen as the holes dug along the water's edge suddenly made sense. "You're a brave kid, Nakai. Someday this will be a good story to tell your buddies around the campfire."

Nakai frowned. "I'm never going back to that campfire in the cave. And I want my friends to get out, too. The Shepherd does bad things to them."

Alika met Sophie's gaze over the boy's prone body. "We will make sure nothing bad happens to you. Or them," Alika promised, his blood heating up at the thought of some pedophile messing with this tough kid and his friends. "Be sure to say something about this to the first responders when they get here." He handed Sophie a few glow sticks. "I need the flashlight to get back, but this ought to keep you going until I get the rescue team to this location."

Sophie cracked the glow sticks, and Nakai cringed even from

their soft green glow. "It's just as well you have time to get used to this level of light," she told the boy softly, stroking his greasy, filthy hair. Alika felt a twinge in his chest at the sight of her tenderness toward this brave, broken kid.

He squelched it by standing and pointing the flashlight down the tunnel. "I'll be right back with help. I'll see you two shortly."

Sophie stood as well, and he stiffened with surprise when she hugged him.

She felt as good as he remembered, springy and strong in his arms. He relaxed, letting his guard down, absorbing the moment, then released her with an effort. "See you soon."

Alika walked as rapidly as he darted back the way he had come. Looking ahead, the column of light that marked the hole they'd come in through burned his eyes. He tried not to imagine what Nakai had been through in the days since he fell down here into utter blackness.

Reaching the opening, Alika took a moment to let his eyes adjust, grasping the knotted rope, and then hauled himself rapidly out of the hole. He grasped the crumbling earthen edge and lifted himself up and out into light that seemed way too bright, even though evening streaked the sky.

Alika blinked, looking around in surprise.

A ring of armed teenagers, radiating hostility, faced him.

CHAPTER THIRTY-THREE

SOPHIE MOVED the three glow sticks Alika had left them off to the side where their light would not cause Nakai more distress. "How are you doing with that protein bar?"

Nakai burped in answer. "I feel a little sick."

Sophie's stomach was a little queasy as well, thinking of the boy eating live worms. She held a water bottle out to Nakai. "Would you like a sip? Maybe it will help."

"No, thanks." The boy's eyes had closed, and even in the greenish light of the glow stick, Sophie could see how pale he was.

He was in shock. She wondered if he was losing blood through the leg that was buried under the boulders. She leaned back stealthily with a glowing stick in her hand to check for any seepage; there was none.

Hopefully the leg was just broken. *What a thing to have to think!*

Sophie stroked the boy's hair and felt him relax after her touch. He actually seemed like he might be falling asleep. Anything that took him away from the current suffering seemed like a good thing.

Her thoughts wandered back to that moment when she had spotted Alika, striding toward them as rapidly as the rough terrain would allow, flashlight swinging. The surge of happiness and endorphins had been too much to ignore, an addicting jolt of well-being that flushed her whole body.

Sophie shook her head, briskly, shooing the thoughts away like irritating flies. *She'd just been feeling relief that help was on its way.*

Alika's flashlight disappeared, masked by that bend in the tunnel where she'd almost gotten lost, leaving nothing to see but the dim green glow of the light sticks. She tightened her hands into fists, momentarily giving in to tension and fear as her tired eyes strained to see him—but he was gone, leaving her again. The sense of abandonment was illogical and acute.

Giving in and wallowing in stupid emotion would not help the situation. She knew that more than most. *There was nothing to do but endure what must be endured.*

Sophie lowered herself to lie beside Nakai, warming him with her body.

A few minutes later, Sophie heard something from the direction in which Alika had gone—a flurry of voices.

Shouting.

The cave walls amplified and bounced sound so that she could not tell the source, but she knew it was coming from the entrance to the lava tube. She picked up one of the glow sticks and rose to her feet.

"I'll be right back, Nakai." She strode forward as fast as she could, holding the light out so that its pale, greenish beam could illuminate the ground immediately in front of her. *Whatever was going on ahead didn't sound good.*

She rounded the bend in the tunnel, and saw the vivid column of light that marked the overhead opening. She heard a scream, and a thud, and the roar of a waterfall of soil and dirt. And then, the light went out.

CHAPTER THIRTY-FOUR

THE TALLEST KID, armed with a good-sized buck knife, stepped forward to poke Alika in the chest—but it was the jiggling crossbow in another kid's shaky hands that worried him.

"Hey guys. What's this about?" Alika kept his voice confident and casual.

"You have our friend Nakai down there, and we want him back." The leader of the gang had unusual gray-green eyes. Dreadlocks framed a highly tanned, angular face.

"Yes, my friend and I found Nakai. He's badly injured, and a fire and rescue team are on the way. I'd think you'd want to help us get him out." Alika raised his brows questioningly, even as he bent his knees and cocked his arms, readying for action. *These kids seemed about as stable as a barrel of nitroglycerin.*

The boy glanced at his friends and yelled, "Put him in the hole!" The boy rushed Alika, swiping at him with the knife. "We can't let them get out and talk about the Shepherd!"

The boys swarmed Alika, slamming him with their bodies and trying to push him backward into the lava tube's opening.

Alika burst into motion, taking down the leader with a quick uppercut to the jaw, kicking back another kid, and slamming a third, knocking him backward into the hole. Alika felt a sting of fire on the back of his arm, and spotted the crossbow's bolt quivering in a nearby tree. He grabbed the shooter by the back of the neck and shoved, sending him sprawling ass over teakettle to fetch up against one of the boulders.

One kid remained. The boy stared at Alika, eyes wide and terrified, and raised his hands. Alika flipped the boy's shirt off over his head and in several quick twists had the kid's arms secured behind his back. He pushed the teen up against one of the boulders and settled him there.

The kid he'd knocked into the lava tube opening was climbing out, his face red with the effort of climbing the rope—but he gave a sudden cry as the crumbling earthen edge began to collapse.

All the activity around the opening must have loosened the rocks and soil and broken the thin wall of lava, because a sudden rush of falling earth and stone swept the teen down and out of sight. The earth trembled and roared ominously as the opening collapsed, a pouf of dust rising like a djinn.

"Holy shit!" Alika rushed to the edge of the pit, almost falling into the jumbled depression that showed where the boy had disappeared. The rim crumbled beneath his feet, and Alika scrambled back, grabbing a sturdy tree branch for balance. He looked wildly around, and gestured to the kid he'd just restrained. "Your friend is buried in there! Let's try to get him out before he suffocates!"

The boy, wide-eyed, scrambled to his feet awkwardly and Alika ripped the restraining shirt off his hands. "Get your friends to help! I'll check if the rope he was holding onto is still secured to the boulder."

The boy hurried to help his groaning friends to their feet as Alika rushed to the boulder he'd tied the line to. Reaching over, he tugged at the cord, and it began to pull out of the dirt. He stopped pulling and checked the rock's stability by pushing at it. The boulder was still solid. He turned, looking for help.

The tall kid with the gray-green eyes, pale now beneath his tan, stood next to him. "Is Eric dead?"

"He will be if we can't get him out of this landslide, fast," Alika said. "I'm too heavy to go out there into the fall area. I want us to make a human chain. We'll each hold onto each other and use the cord to track down to him, and for backup. The lightest of you will go out first and dig down, following the rope, and try to get to your friend. It's his only chance and it might already be too late."

The boy gave a brief nod and turned to the others, showing his leadership skills as he barked, "Emilio! You're out in front!" The remaining boys scrambled to follow directions, and in moments Emilio crawled down the rope headfirst into the pit, using the rope as a guide, digging with his hands as the boys, one clinging to the next with Alika holding up the end, stabilized him.

It couldn't have been longer than five minutes, but it felt like an eternity to Alika as he held onto the tall kid's belt, learning his name was Keo. He anchored Keo as the boy held onto another named Payton, then Raymond, then finally Emilio.

"I think I've got him!" Emilio yelled. "I can feel his hair!"

"Dig, dig!" Alika yelled. "Get Eric some air!"

It wasn't long before Emilio had got the dirt and rocks away from Eric's head. The boy had instinctively covered his head with his arms, making a shallow pocket of air. He'd passed out but soon came around as Emilio slapped his cheeks.

Sweating and straining, Alika pulled the human chain back onto solid ground. Working together they extracted Eric from the loose fall of pebbles and dirt.

They all collapsed, panting in exhaustion, around the pit. Alika's whole body trembled and his shirt was soaked with sweat as he watched filthy, bruised Eric crying as he was hugged by his friends.

His discarded walkie-talkie squawked from inside the backpack he'd cast aside when the confrontation broke out. "Dragonfly, come in. This is Search and Rescue. We've arrived in Kalalau. We're at your bird and looking for directions. Come in, Dragonfly."

Alika scrambled to his feet. He hadn't had time to think of what was happening to Sophie and Nakai; *they must be terrified.* He ran to the backpack, retrieved the handheld, and pushed the Talk button. "Dragonfly here. Things are a little more complicated than I originally thought. We need you down here ASAP."

Alika arranged to meet the rescuers at the turnoff to the encampment. When he lowered the walkie, he looked at the circle of watching boys. A long moment passed, and finally Keo, the leader, extended a hand.

"I'm sorry for what we tried to do."

Alika shook the boy's filthy hand. "I'm not going to take you all down and tie you up—I'm too tired right now for that. I guess I don't expect you to be here when I get back with the Search and Rescue team, but if you stay, I promise we'll get you a better situation than wherever it is you're living. It's up to you."

The boy inclined his head, and the others nodded, but Alika didn't expect to see any of them again. He turned and forced his tired body into a run toward the main trail. *Sophie and Nakai needed him.*

CHAPTER THIRTY-FIVE

SOPHIE STOOD STOCK STILL, afraid to move, afraid to know what she had seen and heard even as the last tremors of the rockfall settled. The smell of freshly turned earth filled her nose.

She felt dizzy.

The tunnel had just collapsed. *The way out was closed.*

"Sandy?" The disturbance had woken the boy. Nakai's voice vibrated with terror. She was torn between returning to the frightened kid and investigating what lay ahead.

Finding out what had happened was more important to their survival.

Sophie turned back, calling out, "I'm all right, Nakai. Just relax. I'm investigating a little landslide that happened."

Nakai wouldn't be able to see around the bend in the tunnel to the disaster that had occurred. No sense in adding to his fear.

"Come back soon!" The kid's voice wobbled.

"I'll be right back." Sophie injected her voice with cheerfulness and authority.

"And I'll just be kicking it over here." Yes, Nakai was a brave kid.

Having been so brave on his own, now that rescue was in sight, he must now be feeling all the feelings he hadn't let himself have before. Sophie could almost hear Dr. Kinoshita's voice in her mind explaining what the boy was going through.

Sophie held her glow stick up and forged ahead. She identified several more sticks that Alika had dropped on his way to them, but left them where they were so they could provide illumination for anyone coming to rescue her and Nakai. She refused to think of any alternative to that. Refused to think of the rest of the tunnel collapsing, or that something had happened to Alika so that he could not bring them help.

A giant pile of dirt and rock almost blocked the tunnel. The hole they had come in through had collapsed, as she had suspected. Sophie's stomach dropped. *Had Alika been buried in the fall?*

But even if he was somehow disabled, the first responders were on their way. The people in the encampment would direct them to Sophie's area, and from there it was just a matter of time until they found the collapsed lava tube.

Rescue was just a matter of time, and patience.

She sure hoped that rescue came before the glow sticks ran out—and she refused to think of Alika injured or trapped. No. He was fine, but his weight must have collapsed the fragile wall of the lava tube as he climbed out. She refused to imagine anything else.

Returning to Nakai, Sophie moved the three glow sticks to where she could get a better look at him, while trying not to disturb him with the light. "Is that protein bar staying down better now?"

Nakai burped again. "I still feel sick."

Sophie's stomach was still queasy, too. She hadn't eaten much lately either, but they both needed energy. She quietly consumed one of the protein bars and followed it up with a bottle of water. She held the bottle out to Nakai. "You need to try to drink some water. It should help settle your stomach."

The boy's eyes had closed again, and he shook his head. He still looked really pale. Sophie knelt beside him.

. . .

NAKAI LIFTED his head to gaze at her, his eyes wide and blank in the green glow of the sticks. "We're not getting rescued right away, are we?"

"We are definitely getting rescued. But you're right, it might be a little longer than we had hoped." She stroked his hair, straightening it, feeling a crust of blood on his scalp. It made her heart twist that he had been through so much and still had to endure so much more.

"How long do glow sticks last?"

Sophie laughed. "We must have a mind meld. I was just thinking the same thing. I believe these usually last four to six hours."

"And just when I was getting used to having some light," Nakai said sleepily, and turned his head away from her.

There was nothing to be done but wait. Worrying wasn't going to make the time go by any faster; in fact, it could use up energy resources she might need. Sophie lay down beside the boy, pressed against him so her body would warm his chilled flesh. She couldn't relax into sleep. Nakai slept, though it was a light and troubled sleep marked by frequent twitches and low moans. The exhaustion of pain and ordeal had caught up to him, and with the resilience of youth, his body had simply shut down.

Sophie had no such escape. Her mind cycled through scenarios, trying to figure a way out.

Even if they lost the glow sticks' light, they would be fine. Of all the people in the world, they two were best equipped to live through an extended period in total darkness without losing their minds. That didn't mean she wanted to go through that.

And what about Ginger, tied at the camp? And oh God, Alika, that magnificent body he'd worked so hard to regain, crushed and smothered... Or trapped, partway in and partway out as Nakai was, with escape hours or days away.

"Please no. Please let Alika be okay," Sophie whispered. These were the times she wished she had a clearer sort of faith, but if there was a God and S/he was merciful...

Sophie pressed closer to the boy, and draped an arm across his back, comforting herself as much as him as she did so.

Her anxious thoughts turned to friends and family.

Her father must be frantic; she didn't know if he'd received her text that she was okay, and now more time had gone by without any communication.

Marcella must be so angry. Having to track down Sophie via a clue at her apartment and send Alika to Kaua'i to get her for her own legal proceeding was above and beyond the call of duty—especially when Marcella already felt betrayed that Sophie had never told her about the Ghost.

Hopefully, when this was all over, they could meet somewhere and discuss everything. Marcella would see that Sophie's position had been impossible.

And that reminded Sophie of Connor.

Her whole body contorted involuntarily as she thought of Connor.

His betrayal was by far the worst. Why hadn't he simply told her that he could not give up his "mission"? Why had he given her reason to hope? And worst of all, how could he have let her grieve his death, when he'd had the opportunity to send her a confidential message? His explanation that he'd wanted to let her move on felt woefully inadequate.

Sophie still had the software program he used for his vigilantism: a program that could hack the phones of gangsters and send them messages, supposedly from each other; a program that appeared able to penetrate the best security and turn it against itself. The Ghost program might be even more powerful than her own DAVID program.

And that software was sitting on a hard drive at the bottom of her backpack, along with her satellite-enabled laptop.

She probably couldn't get a signal out from this far underground, but she had not been able to crack the Ghost program's security the last time she tried. Perhaps this was the perfect thing to do to pass the time until her laptop battery ran out.

Sophie eased away from the boy and fetched the backpack, resting her back against a boulder and unzipping it. She took out that laptop and turned to face Nakai so that the faint glow of the screen wouldn't wake him. She plugged in the external hard drive Connor had left her in the safe deposit box, and pulled up the Ghost program.

The login screen blinked at her blankly. She checked the Post-it app on her screen with all the combinations she had already tried. She'd run through the days of every first she and Connor had shared: their first date, the first time they made contact online, even the day Connor had taken a bullet to save her from a murderous perp on one of her cases. She couldn't think of anything new to try.

Connor had given her the software with the expectation that she would use it; therefore, it made sense that she should be able to crack its security code. *But if not, there was always the usual way.* Sophie opened one of her code-breaking programs and set it to work running combinations.

Now it was just a matter of time. She watched the counter tick through letters, first, as it tried them for each spot. She felt an unpleasant emotion in the area of her stomach. *Disappointment.*

Sophie was disappointed that Connor hadn't customized the login, given it some personal meaning. And here she was, buried underground, and there was no way he could help her.

As much as Sophie had told herself that she wanted nothing more to do with Connor, knowing that a powerful criminal mastermind loved her had given her just a little more confidence to step off into the unknown. "I can always find you," he had said. *And she believed him.* Even here, even now…she would gamble that he at least knew her general location. If too much time went by, Connor would come looking for her. And he, of all people, was the most equipped to find her—with not only his tech savvy but also his physical skills and unlimited financial resources.

Jake could probably find her, too.

TOBY NEAL

Her partner was another person who was likely angry with her right now. She had cut him off with hardly a goodbye. He didn't deserve that, no matter how unsettling he was in her life. His friendship, loyalty, and many skills had earned her confidence and trust.

Leaning against Jake's warm hard bulk at Connor's mock funeral had been some of the best moments in those nightmare days.

She missed his physicality, his frequent laugh, his enthusiasm, energy, and potent personality. There were many things about him she didn't miss, but not his reliability in a crisis. Sophie squirmed with embarrassment, remembering that moment in Shank Miller's kitchen when she had almost flung herself on him.

Thank God, they had never so much as kissed. She had a sense that if they ever did, it would be hard to stop.

She was exhausted by her emotions. How could she have attraction and feelings for such different men? Was something wrong with her? Had Assan broken something in her that "normal" women had? Was she so damaged that she couldn't recognize a good partner for herself? Because so far, she hadn't been able to…

The spiral of negative thoughts heralded the beating batwings of depression. Sophie watched the decryption counter whirl by in the dark, unseeing, until letters began appearing. Her eyes widened as she recognized the beginning of words. A phrase was emerging: **I*love* had appeared.

Sophie halted the code breaker program. She typed in, **I*love*you*Sophie**

"Yakish fool!" Sophie exclaimed, as the login window shimmered away in a cascade of ribbons and confetti and the Ghost software opened. "I want to hate you, Connor!"

Connor had personalized the login. She would have to change that code straightaway. Still, it gave her a warm feeling to watch the last of the ribbons spiral out of the screen.

Sophie was gazing at a world map. Red, pulsing markers were displayed in various areas across the globe, most of them in densely populated cities like Beijing, London, Paris, São Paulo, Los Angeles, and New York.

These probably were targets for his brand of justice that he had either already eliminated or had on his radar to manipulate. She was almost afraid to open any of them. She forced herself to choose one that was centered over Honolulu, and click it.

No Internet available flashed on the screen.

So this was a cloud-based program. She wondered what was stored in the depths of the program, what root protocols were encapsulated in the heavy external hard drive she had retrieved from the safe deposit box. She abandoned the opening screen and searched for the program specs. Fingers flying, she penetrated the layers of the program, investigating the base code.

Like her own DAVID program, the Ghost was a data mining and security firewall disabling program, appearing to work by searching out personal information, then digging in to extract details of identity and communication as well as financial sources. Unlike DAVID, which searched keywords and compiled confidence ratios on a given possibility, the Ghost could burrow out communications and then send new ones from its victims like a programmable virus.

Sophie found a subroutine that harvested bank account information, and frowned to see that pennies were being harvested off of thousands of accounts and rerouted to other accounts.

She had no way to look up where the numbers were coming from and going to, but she would be willing to bet that the Ghost was skimming money from drug dealers and rerouting it to either himself or some worthy cause. That was just the kind of thing Connor would love to do. He was probably using Security Solutions as the front to get all of those gangsters' business, being paid for protection of those accounts up front.

Oh, how Connor would love the game of being hired for security and then using that access to rob unscrupulous clients. She could picture the gleam in his eye as he set up his clients to be fleeced, and ultimately, to die.

There was nothing more she could learn about the Ghost software without accessing the Cloud, and the internal conflict of thinking about Connor and his "mission" was too disturbing. Sophie shut down the laptop, and glanced over at the glow sticks.

They looked dimmer. Maybe it was her imagination.

CHAPTER THIRTY-SIX

THE SEARCH and rescue team met Alika at the junction between the main trail and the turnoff toward the encampment. Striding toward him were two sturdy young men in dark blue uniforms, lugging a portable gurney. They were followed by a female EMT carrying a medical case.

Alika introduced himself. "There has been a further complication. The hole we discovered to access the lava tube has collapsed, and my companion is stuck down there with the victim. There's no way to tell how stable the area is for further digging, and we don't have any equipment. Do you have anything for excavating back at your chopper?"

"Yes, we do. We should also call for further backup in case heavier equipment is needed." The team leader pulled his handheld radio off his belt and called it in to the pilot, still at the aircraft.

A tall, well-built, wild-haired man wearing a sarong appeared on the trail from the encampment. "Need help? Is something wrong?" Several others clustered behind him. They must be people from the encampment.

"We found a boy who was missing. He'd fallen into a lava tube. My friend is with him, but the opening collapsed," Alika explained.

The man glanced at his companions. "Enola's boy. Nakai." He turned back. "We'd like to help. Put us to work."

The leader of the rescue team looked the man up and down. "I'm Captain Hamilton. You are?"

"Tiger. We're camping here on sovereign Hawaiian lands." The man eyed the rescue team defiantly. "But we look after our own, and Nakai and his mother are a part of our community. We'd like to help."

"Well, since we're not expecting another chopper out here for at least a few hours, why don't you help us carry down some more equipment from our helicopter, and we'll assess the situation at the site? You can also bring anything you have at your camp that's useful for digging."

The men set off back up the trail, as the EMT approached Alika. "You've got some scrapes and bruises. How did that happen?"

Alika shrugged. He had no intention of saying anything about the teens' attack. "It was rough getting down into the tube."

"Let me patch you up while we wait for the equipment." The woman went to work with gauze and ointment, and had Alika's swellings and wounds treated by the time the rescue team, Tiger, and a couple of his minions returned. They carried a foldable ladder, ropes, shovels and even a portable pickaxe along with other, unknown equipment.

Alika led the group back to the site, and as he'd suspected, the boys were gone. Alika pointed to the disturbed earth around the rope that was dangling down into what had been the opening into the lava tube as the group ringed the landslide. "I had some help from some teenagers in the area, because one of them was caught in the dirt fall after I climbed out to go call you. We held onto the rope and dug down to get the kid out. They didn't hang around for the rescue effort."

"How far away from this opening are your friend and the injured boy?" Captain Hamilton asked.

"Not close. Several hundred yards away, around a curve in the tunnel. They should be okay if they stay back, and Sandy's smart. She won't be trying to dig her way out or anything. She knows we're coming."

Captain Hamilton nodded. He gestured for everyone to move back from the edge. "Let's set up a perimeter. We should not pressure the area if we can help it. Since you've already started excavating where your rope is attached to that boulder, it seems like it might be safe for us to continue to expand that opening. We can follow the rope downward and use these stabilizers to hold the tunnel open." He took out a heavy-duty plastic ring, wide enough to crawl through. The other staffer took one end and the ring telescoped open into a long, sturdy plastic tube. "These can be used to provide more stability to the hole, as long as it's not too deep. How far was it to the bottom?"

"Couple feet over my head, so around eight feet down."

"We should be okay then. Let's make a human chain and fill buckets with soil, and pass them back to be dumped. We have enough people that we can rotate out when we get tired."

The next hour passed quickly as the impromptu rescue team dug and moved soil. Captain Hamilton continued to direct, and the reinforced tube followed the digging as it went down, expanding the tunnel.

Eventually Alika needed a rest. Sitting under a nearby guava tree, resting his back against the slender trunk, he sipped a bottle of water one of the campers had brought, and thought about the situation with the boys.

Someone was going to have to deal with those runaways and what was going on in that cave with the Shepherd, whoever he was. Maybe Sophie would have an idea what to do once she got out.

Finally, the crew broke through the dirt fall into open space, and the last segment of the collapsible support tube was slid into place. Alika stood, heading for the opening, but Captain Hamilton held up a hand. "Authorized personnel only. This area is too unstable for civilians."

Two of the smallest rescue team members made their way carefully down through the chute. Alika had given them all the information he had about the boy's condition and his current state, but the tube was too narrow to admit the gurney. Alika watched tensely as the rescuers were handed down a first aid kit and close work equipment to move the rocks off of Nakai's leg.

Everyone participating in the rescue effort and most of the encampment waited anxiously outside the barrier as reports were relayed via walkie to Captain Hamilton.

The moment Alika saw Sophie's filthy face rise up out of the pit he wanted to haul her out and kiss her. He restrained himself, instead taking her hand to pull her out of the opening and lift her out onto her feet. "Thank God you're okay."

Sophie embraced him, pressing her face into his chest, her arms tight around his back. She shut her eyes as he caressed her short, springy curls with one hand and held her close with the other. He'd forgotten how good she felt in his arms—he'd tried to, at least.

"It sure took you long enough," she whispered.

"I know. It seemed like forever."

"Nakai is in bad shape. I hope they fly him straight to the hospital." Sophie spoke into his filthy shirt. He squeezed her close.

"I'm sure that's the plan." Alika let go of Sophie reluctantly, and the two of them turned to watch the injured boy be carefully moved up through the escape tunnel. Nakai moaned as he was lifted out, holding his arms over his eyes. Even the waning evening light must be too harsh for his eyes to handle. His leg had been splinted but it was a bloody mess, and he shrieked when it touched the ground.

Sophie rushed to Nakai, touching his shoulder and murmuring in his ear as the team settled the child on the gurney. Her voice seemed to calm the boy as the team worked to stabilize his leg and hook up an IV as the circle of concerned-looking campers watched.

"Mom? Where are you, Mom?" Nakai cried. Alika felt his chest tighten at the boy's anguish that his mother was clearly nowhere to be found.

Sophie, kneeling beside Nakai, hushed the boy with tender whispers. "I'll let her know you're okay."

Alika waited until the rescue team was on its way up the trail, with several campers also helping carry the boy's gurney as they headed back toward the two choppers. He pulled Sophie aside, waving to Captain Hamilton that they would catch up.

The EMTs had said that Nakai was being taken to the hospital on Oahu, because the flight was only forty minutes further than it would be to go to Wilcox Hospital, which wasn't as well equipped for children. "Do you want to follow them to Oahu?"

"I'm not leaving until I deal with the Shepherd. We need to call Kaua'i Police Department."

Alika met Sophie's angry eyes, startled. He glanced over at the backs of the rescue team, already ascending the trail. "Don't you think we'd be better off accompanying Nakai to the hospital? Getting cleaned up, getting some rest? I don't know about you, but I'm pretty wiped out right now, and it's nearly dark. I propose either we spend the night here at your camp and fly out tomorrow, or we fly out tonight and spend the night with friends or family on Oahu. You can do the deposition that Marcella is so worried about, and then, I'll bring you back with the police and proper Social Services authorities. Right now, I don't know what we have to offer these kids." Alika told Sophie about the boys' attack on him and how it had caused the rockfall. "I didn't tell the captain what happened because I didn't want a police raid on the cave before we were ready to offer those kids a better situation." Alika pushed a hand into his hair, shoveling it off his brow. "Do you know anyone in Social Services to help get them a group foster home so they can stay together?" The stress of the situation was sapping the last of his strength.

"This is a police matter. Those boys attacked you, and they are being abused by a pedophile. It isn't up to us to determine the right way to approach the situation," Sophie's voice was stiff and cold. "We just need to get it stopped. Right now, if possible."

Alika stepped back, his eyes widening. "I thought you cared about those boys."

"I do care about them. And that's why I want to see them moved out of that cave and the Shepherd locked up. You should have just told Captain Hamilton what the boys did. He could have called in a team to deal with them and that perp in the cave. As it is, I haven't had time to report what Nakai said or do anything about it."

They both glanced up the trail. The rest of the group had gone already.

The two faced off. Filthy, hollow-eyed with stress and exhaustion, she was still gorgeous as she put her hands on her hips. "You're a civilian. You don't know how these things work. This is clearly a police matter and our job is to report it and get it dealt with."

"A lot of times, here in Hawaii, we like to handle things more casually, if possible," Alika said. "You've only been here five years, and all that time, until now, you were in high rises and the FBI." His neck felt hot. "You don't know the local culture."

"I don't know what's 'local' about those boys trying to throw you into the pit and bury all of us alive," Sophie said. "And yet, they are just children, doing their master's bidding. The Shepherd is the real criminal." She paused, looked at the sky, and sighed. "You are right about one thing. This is probably not the right time to act on this. I have a dog, and she needs attention, and we both need rest and sustenance. Let's go back to my camp, eat something and clean up a bit, and then take Ginger and your chopper and go to Oahu. I will report what I saw and heard to the authorities, you can also make a statement, and we will help organize a team to come back out here and deal with the boys and the Shepherd."

Sophie turned and walked up the trail.

"Damn, girl." Alika shook his head. "You da boss."

CHAPTER THIRTY-SEVEN

ALIKA HAD OBTAINED the information from air traffic control that there was a helipad on top of the apartment building where Sophie's father, Ambassador Francis Smithson, lived. Sophie had lived there, too, for the first five years of her time in Hawaii, but the swanky building in an upscale area of Honolulu looked unfamiliar from above as Sophie watched them descend. The helicopter wove back and forth in an updraft as it lowered to land upon the big bold X marking the touchdown area.

Sophie's stomach churned from the crossing: winds were strong out of the north, and Oahu was over an hour away from Kaua'i, northernmost of the main Hawaiian chain. She wasn't usually queasy, but the heavy bumping, combined with a belly weighed down by just a protein bar or two in the last eight hours, made her both dizzy and ill.

Alika seemed unaffected by their travails. Sophie sneaked a glance at his handsome profile. His hands were steady on the collective, his eyes scanning both the ground and the bank of instruments in front of them.

It was so good to be with him again, no matter the circumstances.

Somehow, unlike Jake or Connor, he was both peaceful and energizing to be with.

· Alika set the chopper down with no more than a gentle rocking. Sophie looked through the Bell Jet Ranger's bubble of glass panel and spotted her father exiting the metal doorway that marked the entrance to the building. She took off her helmet as Alika cut the engine.

"I did the best I could, given the bumpy wind conditions," Alika said. "I hope you feel okay."

"Nothing a good dinner and some time on the ground won't improve." Sophie smiled at him. "Dad said he had a good meal ready and waiting for us." She indicated her father with a head nod.

"Excellent." Alika's white teeth flashed. "I could eat a whole imu pig myself, right now."

They got out of the chopper as Ginger barked a happy greeting to her father. Alika circled the chopper, fastening anchor clips to the struts while Sophie hurried to hug Frank. Ginger wound her leash around both of their legs.

"My girl." Frank Smithson had the best hug, tight and strong, but allowing space for Sophie to rest her head on his shoulder and snuggle in. Her father had been her rock amid the stormy seas of Sophie's mother and her chronic depression, and later, Sophie's disastrous marriage.

Frank patted Sophie's back and she broke away. She gestured to Alika as he approached, carrying both of their backpacks. "Dad, you remember Alika? My MMA coach from Fight Club."

"Of course I do. Good to see you again, Alika. Glad you could help get Sophie home." Her father turned to face Sophie, and this time his gaze was chastising. "You gave us all quite a scare, young lady. And you're not out of hot water with that thing with your ex."

"You mean whether or not I'll face a murder charge for killing him, Dad?" Sophie felt driven to keep saying the unspeakable. "I did it, and I'm not sorry. I did it because he was going to torture and kill me. Once more, and for the record, I have nothing to be ashamed of.

I won't do jail time for him, no matter what the DA decides." Her voice had gained in ferocity.

Frank studied her for a long moment. "Okay." Her father's tone was mild. "But there's no excuse for blowing off your old man. We had an agreement—you were to contact me every three days."

"I know. And I tried. But there's not even text messaging available in Kalalau."

Alika cleared his throat awkwardly. "Rumor has it, Ambassador, that there is some dinner to be had." He patted his flat belly as it gave a loud growl. "And I am very interested in that possibility."

"Of course!" Frank turned and clapped Alika on the shoulder. "Sophie tells me you had quite an adventure rescuing a young boy trapped underground. I look forward to hearing all about it."

MUCH LATER, Sophie walked Alika to the door of the apartment. Lacquered in red, flanked by tall, carved porcelain urns, the entry of the penthouse was stunning with its floor-to-ceiling, full-length windows along one wall. Seeing Alika in these familiar surroundings reminded Sophie how much she had enjoyed living there for those solo years. They had enjoyed a delicious Thai curry dinner that her father had prepared, but Alika insisted on leaving.

"You sure you want to go to your friend's house to spend the night?" Sophie asked him. "There's plenty of room. We can make up the couch."

"No, thank you. As I told Frank, I have a bedroom available with friends that help me with managing Fight Club. I'm all set."

An awkward silence fell. They could hear the splashing sounds of Frank loading the dishwasher in the sleek, modern kitchen. "Got to say, this is the first time I can remember having a US ambassador cook and clean up dinner for me," Alika said.

Sophie shrugged. "My father enjoys domestic activities when he's not working. Says the simplicity restores his mind."

"Well, keep me posted on how the deposition goes tomorrow."

Sophie had contacted Marcella, and her friend had left a message during dinner that Sophie was just in time; the deposition was the following day, and Marcella would pick her up for it in the morning at nine a.m. Sophie was looking forward to seeing Marcella; she had fences to mend with her friend from the FBI.

Alika reached out, touched a bit of her short-cropped hair. His voice was low. "I haven't had time to tell you that you look as beautiful as ever to me."

Sophie swayed toward him. "You don't have to lie to me."

"I would never lie to you." Alika slid his hands up to her shoulders slowly so that she could pull away if she wanted to, but she didn't want to. She was the one to lean into his space, tipping up her face to kiss him.

They fit together perfectly, as they always had. She shut her eyes and gave herself over to sensation and emotion. Like diving into a familiar swimming hole on a hot day, kissing Alika was both refreshing and familiar. The kiss felt safe, as did his arms around her, but his touch also stirred heat along her nerve endings.

She couldn't help a flash of memory of being in Connor's arms. *Safe was not something she'd ever felt there.*

And yet, both Connor and Alika had hurt her, each in a different way...

Alika was the one to break the kiss, stepping back and stroking her bare arms. His eyes were such a warm brown. His calloused hands raised goose bumps on her skin. "I didn't mean for that to happen. I hope you're okay."

"It's just a kiss," Sophie said, stepping back. "And I hope *you're* okay with that."

Alika winced. "I guess I deserve that."

The splashing noises had ceased in the kitchen. Frank came to the door, wiping his hands on a towel. "Sophie's tied up with the deposition tomorrow, but I hope you will meet me late afternoon for a beer at my favorite pub."

Alika nodded respectfully to the older man. "Sure. You have my number, just let me know when. I'm going by my gym to check up on things tomorrow. I'll be giving Sophie a ride back to Kalalau so we can deal with the aftermath of the situation over there. I'll look forward to talking with you both later." He picked up his backpack and stepped through the door. "Take care. I'll see you soon."

"Goodbye." Sophie closed the door softly behind him.

She wondered what her father was up to. This was the first time he'd shown any interest in a man she was seeing—not that there had been many. Her father had gone back into the kitchen, so Sophie was able to stand for a moment, savoring the tingle in her lips and body.

She was off men, forever. Alika made that hard to remember.

Sophie bid her father good night and went into her old bedroom. A little more than a week ago she had been here, packing the last of her clothing and personal items before her hiking trip. Frank must've had the maid come in, because the room was pristine but for Ginger, looking guilty, lying on the jade silk coverlet.

Sophie clapped her hands and scolded the dog, still damp from a bath Frank had given her upon their arrival. "Look at this. You've ruined my comforter."

Frank frowned from the doorway. "Bad dog!"

Ginger slunk off the bed and out of the room. Frank pointed to the dog bed he kept ready for the Lab by the couch. Ginger got in, circled and lay down. Frank petted her head.

"I have to make some phone calls, okay, Dad?" He nodded, used to her working from home, and Sophie closed the door of her bedroom. She sat down at the rig she'd left behind, booting it up as she called Jake. She left a message at his brusque voicemail recording. He wouldn't know this number, and, like her, he didn't answer unknown numbers. The phone rang minutes later as she removed the hard drive containing the Ghost software and plugged it into her desktop computer.

"Where the hell have you been?" Jake Dunn was what Americans called a "force of nature." Sophie heard him breathing through his nose as if he were trying to calm himself. She could picture him so clearly: those gunmetal eyes under dark brows intent and his big, restless, muscled body, always ready to erupt into action, probably pacing around in agitation.

"Hello, Jake. I knew you would be worried, and so I called as soon as I could. I hope you are well." She didn't owe Jake anything; he had no claim on her other than friendship and their work partnership, but he had always acted both attached and overprotective. *That was his problem, not hers.* "I went hiking on Kaua'i. I encountered a situation. It got complicated."

"You always encounter a situation." Her partner blew out a breath. "Shank Miller has been concerned. You're his favorite security agent."

"And Shank is my favorite rock star." Miller had a beach house on Maui, and had recently had complications with a persistent stalker. That case had drawn Jake and Sophie to Maui for some months. "How are things over there?"

"I'm almost done hiring the last of Miller's permanent security team, and I'm back on Oahu in a few days. When can we get together?"

Sophie looked down at the silky carpet between her bare toes. She rubbed a foot, still a little tender from all that time in her hiking boots, across the expensive nap. "I'm here on Oahu and staying with my father. Tomorrow I'll give my deposition regarding Assan Ang's death. And then I'm going right back to Kalalau."

"What about your job with Security Solutions?"

"I tendered my resignation directly to Sheldon Hamilton." She had, in a manner of speaking. But she still needed to call Kendall Bix, her immediate supervisor, and formalize things.

"So, what are you doing for work?"

"I'm not sure. I have a little savings; I'm just going to do some exploring. Off the grid."

"You know, I've always wanted to do something like that myself and never made the time. Let me know if you need anything, or ever want a hiking buddy." The strained quality of Jake's voice told her how concerned he was. He cleared his throat. "But after all you've been through, a break is in order. Just don't be a stranger, okay?"

"I will never be a stranger to you, Jake. I owe you my life." Sophie had needed to say that for a while. "How about you meet Alika, my father and me for a beer after I finish with my deposition? Perhaps Marcella will come too."

"Alika? Who is he?"

"Alika Wolcott is a Kaua'i real estate developer and my former MMA coach. I was dating him before Connor." *No sense hiding anything.*

Silence met this. Then, "I'll be there. This guy I've got to meet."

CHAPTER THIRTY-EIGHT

THE NEXT MORNING, Alika followed his friend and gym manager, Chewy, into the large, dim, barnlike space of Fight Club in downtown Honolulu. He had supported the club when it opened ten years ago, then had eventually bought out the majority partner. Just one of his businesses, the gym had been doing well and turning a profit even in the year he had been absent from it.

Chewy smacked him on the shoulder companionably as Alika surveyed the gym, segmented into different areas by racks of sports and weight equipment. "Fight Club's doing all right without you, but we're all glad you're back."

Alika started as the overhead floodlights burst on suddenly.

The Rocky soundtrack blared out of the gym's large speakers.

"Welcome back, Coach!" A group of Alika's former coaching students and regulars jumped out from behind the raised boxing ring that was the gym's focal point, shouting and firing off party poppers. Confetti showered down from the second-story walkway above, dumped directly on Alika by a mischievously grinning assistant manager.

Alika fought stinging eyes as he was swarmed, hugged, clapped on the back, and lifted up to be jogged around the ring on the shoulders of six sturdy friends.

Chewy oversaw the dispensing of cups of Gatorade from an oversized orange thermos. He led the group in a toast: "To Coach Alika. May he continue to rise to every challenge, come back from every beatdown, and kick ass every day, setting an example for the rest of us like he always has."

Alika gulped at his Gatorade, his throat too tight to swallow, and was obliterated by another round of hugs. A chant of "Speech! Speech! Speech!" started, and he finally slipped between the ropes of the ring and set aside his plastic cup.

"I stand here, damn glad to be alive after last year's attack—and to be able to do this." Alika ripped off his shirt, and ran through a memorized fight sequence, a series of moves borrowed from jiu-jitsu, Muay Thai, and Tae Kwon Do. Through the rapid moves, rolls, kicks, and punches, his leg still ached and a zap of the familiar lightning-like nerve pain shot from his ribs down his arm—*but he was back, and someday he'd be better than ever.*

The applause of friends lifted his spirits as he ended the bout with his arms raised in victory, wishing Sophie was there to see him.

Hours later, Alika sat in his office chair, his legs stretched out and crossed on the corner of the desk. Chewy sat kitty-corner to him, mirroring his pose. They each held a stack of profit and loss reports.

"You've been running this place better than I did," Alika said. "I've been keeping up long-distance, but this is impressive. Who knew that yoga and Zumba would do so well here?"

Chewy, nicknamed Chewbacca for his luxuriant growth of hair and beard, stroked the pelt on his chin. "There were empty hours in the gym when none of our regulars were working out. I surveyed the community and discovered there weren't any of those classes nearby.

We weren't tapping into the resources of the stay-at-home mom demographic. That's no longer the case."

"Very nice. And your addition of pole dance aerobics and expansion of the ladies' boxing coach program seems to be going well."

Chewy's eyes twinkled in the bushy growth of his brows. "Once I realized those pole dancing props could be put up and taken down, I saw a match made in heaven between that class setting up in the boxing ring, and our evening gym rats. You should see all the guys lined up on the stationary bikes and treadmills, watching while those ladies shake it. It's a hoot."

"I guess everyone's getting what they came for, then." Alika put down his report, leaned forward and steepled his fingers. "I think you deserve a cut of our growth. What would you say to a little profit-sharing?"

"Most definitely. Thanks for thinking of it."

"But that welcome home party was a little over-the-top. Just FYI."

"Not at all. The minute I sent out a group text that you were going to be in town for the first time in a year, your students did all the rest. You're missed, Coach."

"Well, I appreciate it, then. I guess. It's been a rough year on Kaua'i, working with a physical therapist and rehab coach just to get back to where I was." Alika gestured to his legs, propped on the desk. "I won't be fighting again any time soon, but I'm glad to be able to do paddling and surfing like I used to."

"You're doing a lot more than that. You had a great set of moves to show us."

Alika dropped his feet and stood. "I'll be back a lot sooner than a year next time. There's someone here I want to keep in touch with."

"Sophie?" Chewy grinned. "Don't blame you a bit. Tell her we miss her, too."

Alika pretended to be looking for a pen in his desk. "We'll see what happens. She's been through a lot, and I'm not the only guy who's into her."

"My money's on you, Alika." Chewy stood. "Well, I'll be picking up sweaty towels in the shower area." He left.

Alika watched him go. If only he was as confident as his friend that Sophie wanted anything to do with him—though that kiss had been promising.

But was he any more ready for a relationship than she was?

He slammed the desk drawer. *Hell yes.* He'd made that decision when he took the Dragonfly to go look for her.

CHAPTER THIRTY-NINE

MARCELLA HAD BEEN lucky enough to find a parallel parking spot in front of Sophie's dad's building. The wide, pretty avenue with its spreading monkeypod trees was quiet in the early morning. She'd texted Sophie on her arrival, and her friend exited the building's glass doors. Wearing a plain white button-down shirt and easy-movement black slacks, Sophie was dressed as she'd been every day for the five years they'd worked together at the FBI, and the sight gave Marcella a pang.

She got out of her Honda Accord and came around to embrace her friend on the sidewalk.

Sophie smelled of sandalwood soap. Her grip was almost bruising on Marcella as the women hugged. "I'm so sorry I just went off without telling you where," Sophie whispered. "It was wrong of me. I was...grieving."

"I know you were." Marcella was glad she'd taken the time to sort through her emotions and let go of her hurt and anger. She held Sophie at arm's length. "You cut your hair off again."

Sophie tugged at her short, dense, dark brown curls self-consciously. "I needed to wear a wig. And—this is easy. Not much to it."

"That's always been a good look for you, scar or no scar." Marcella's Italian mama instincts kicked in as she took in her friend's hollow cheeks. "Really, not much to you anywhere, now. I need to feed you up, girl. You're getting downright skinny. Let's stop by a coffee shop on the way to the law office; I bet you didn't eat breakfast." They got into the Accord and Marcella headed for the nearest Starbucks drive-through. "I'm going to get some carbs, sugar, and caffeine into you. Now tell me everything."

Sophie did, beginning with her decision to go to Kalalau, spurred by a postcard she'd found in the Ghost's office. "It seemed like it was some kind of message. I'd been enjoying myself for the most part, figuring out my camping gear each night, Ginger and I just taking our time and enjoying that incredible place, when this woman literally stumbled into our camp, hysterical over her missing son."

Marcella ordered a large black coffee for herself and tea and a breakfast croissant for Sophie at the drive-through, and listened as her friend unburdened herself about the situation she'd found in that remote valley on Kaua'i. "As soon as I'm done with the deposition, I'm supposed to meet Dad and Alika and Jake for a drink at the Honua Pub. But all I want to do is go see Nakai in the hospital. He must be so afraid with not one familiar face around him."

Marcella glanced at Sophie, concerned by the vibration of emotion in her friend's voice. "Sounds like it really affected you."

Sophie blew out a breath. "I never told you that I was kidnapped when I was seven years old."

Marcella almost put on the brakes. She glanced at the dashboard clock—there was no time to stop and hear the story. "No, you did not. I would have remembered."

"I was taken from my family home in Thailand. The kidnappers snuck in at night, and removed me from my bed." Sophie's voice was flat, as if reciting something memorized. "They kept me in a closet. I was not abused. Each day they took a photo of me holding the daily paper. That was my only human contact. When the payoff came through, the kidnappers left me on the sidewalk in front of a hospital. I hadn't been eating, and I was dehydrated. The hospital took me in, and finally my father and my nanny showed up. The kidnappers had said I would be left in a public place, but not where —so it took a while for anyone to believe my story and contact my family."

Marcella patted Sophie's rigid arm. "Wow, hon. Well, Nakai isn't you. He's older, for one thing, and he's already been through a lot in his short life. He might just be enjoying lying in a clean bed, eating his head off, and watching TV for the first time in months."

Sophie smiled, and her large, dark eyes crinkled a little at the humor. Even with the scar marring her face and no makeup or other adornment, she was beautiful. "I hope you're right. I can see the boy slurping down Jell-O and enjoying cartoons, now that you put it like that."

"You know I'm right."

"Of course. You're always right."

"At last she admits the obvious." Marcella glanced at Sophie, and they both grinned.

Marcella pulled in to the large Honolulu State building beside the courthouse and parked in the lot beneath. She picked up her briefcase as they exited the Accord. "I called Security Solutions' contracted legal counsel for you. I figured since you hadn't officially resigned from the security firm, we might as well utilize their staff."

Sophie smiled gratefully. "Thanks. Though I am not sure that this whole matter comes under the umbrella of my work with them, I'm grateful to have someone to represent me."

"Chang, the DA, is a bit of a pompous ass. I recommend flattering him and letting him think he's in charge, but don't give him any more information than you have to. For instance, I would leave out the part about surveilling Assan in his building. Just tell the part about following a clue that led you there."

"I'm not an idiot," Sophie said crisply. "I have no intention of going to jail for Assan, no matter what the DA tries to charge me with. But that doesn't mean I'm going to advertise it. I know when to keep my mouth shut and play the submissive." Marcella couldn't miss the bitterness in Sophie's tone, and she patted Sophie's arm, unsure how to respond.

"It's going to be fine," she finally said, and mentally crossed her fingers.

THE CONFERENCE ROOM set up for Sophie's deposition was strictly utilitarian. Marcella accompanied Sophie inside, and introduced her friend to Bennie Fernandez, Security Solutions' legal counsel.

Fernandez was a short, round, cherubic man who resembled Santa Claus in an aloha shirt. His face broke into a smile with a lot of teeth as he greeted Marcella. "Fighting on the same side this time, my dear."

"For once, Fernandez." Marcella could not bring herself to smile back at the deceptively cute pit viper of a defense counselor. Fernandez had dragged many an agent and HPD officer through the metaphorical mud in court in the past, and Marcella was never one to forget a slight or injury. "My friend Sophie needs your 'A' game, and you and I both know how good that is."

"I've been looking for a chance to sharpen my teeth on Chang. You can count on me." Fernandez turned to Sophie, giving her his full, intense attention. "Come with me, my dear, and tell me everything that happened, so I can make sure you don't tell that grandstanding poser anything more than strictly necessary."

They left, and Marcella sat in the empty conference room. She took out her phone and thumbed through her contacts.

She knew a detective their mutual friend Lei Texeira had worked with on Kaua'i. Jack Jenkins was still assigned to the north side of the island; maybe he could get out there and investigate the sticky situation in Kalalau that involved not just Nakai, but a whole group of runaway teens. They needed a group foster home for all the boys to go to, and a sensitive investigation into what was really going on in that cave in one of the most remote valleys in all of Hawaii.

CHAPTER FORTY

SOPHIE FELT PHYSICALLY and emotionally better after talking with Fernandez and Marcella, her spirit lightened by unburdening herself, while at the same time anchored by the food her friend had wisely made her eat. She was also bolstered by the hugs her father had given her that morning as she said goodbye to him in the penthouse.

She could do this.

Sophie had nothing to be ashamed of. She would hold her head up, look the DA in the eye, and say as little as possible.

District Attorney Alan Chang was shorter than she expected, with a similar build to the rotund Bennie Fernandez. Watching the two face off was like watching a pair of small plump roosters kick up dust, preparing to fight in the servants' courtyard of her family compound in Thailand.

"I believe you have been apprised of your rights regarding this proceeding and advised that anything you say here can be used against you in any future legal proceeding," Chang said after the formalities had been observed.

Sophie inclined her head and he prompted her to verbalize her responses, reminding her of the transcription recording occurring.

"Let's begin by discussing your relationship with your ex-husband."

"Why don't we stay focused on the events of the date in question, or we will be here all day," Fernandez rebutted. "Keep your questions specific to information you need to verify."

"I am trying to determine whether or not a murder was committed," Chang said. "That means I have to determine intent. And I would like to know Ms. Ang's intent toward her ex-husband, Assan Ang."

"I can answer that. My intent was to get away from him, preserve myself from bodily harm, and carry on a peaceful life without his hostile presence and murderous attacks," Sophie said. All of Chang's features were concentrated in the middle of his face like a round, shiny emoticon caricature. "I'm sure you have read transcripts from the police report I made of the initial attack by hired professionals trying to kidnap me from Shank Miller's estate on Maui."

"Those transcripts provided some useful background, but that specific attack was never definitively linked to Assan Ang."

"Do you know of any other murderous felons who escaped federal custody who might want to grab and kill me?" Sophie felt the back of her neck getting hot. She calmed herself consciously with relaxation breathing.

"We are not here to determine Assan Ang's intention toward *you.* We are here to attempt to determine *your* intention toward *him.* So why don't we begin again. Tell me why you broke into Paradise Treasures Gallery and the series of events that followed after you did. "

Sophie looked to Fernandez for direction, and the little lawyer inclined his head. "I had a clue tying Assan to the gallery that the FBI and Interpol were not privy to." Speaking slowly and deliberately, Sophie described the series of events that had led to her final confrontation with her ex.

"And why was that original information—that clue you referred to—not turned over to the proper authorities?"

Sophie kept her voice even. "The information was something

only I would know—a familiar bank login code. I did not trust the proper authorities, as you call them, to handle the situation with the delicacy it deserved."

"And how delicate was damaging the locking mechanism for the building's security, breaking into the building, and then confronting Mr. Ang in the apartment on the top floor?"

"Ms. Ang declines to answer this question, pleading her Fifth Amendment rights," Bennie Fernandez inserted smoothly. "She has already admitted to breaking and entering and trespassing on private property, and no charges are being pressed against her." Fernandez reached inside his jacket and produced an envelope. "This contains a letter of apology and a check made out to Paradise Treasures and Maggie Kennedy, the owner, for damages."

Sophie had signed the letter and check, already filled out from Fernandez & Associates' private account, during their quick prep session. *The lawyer was that good.*

"This is neither here nor there." Chang pushed the letter and check aside. "What I want to know is, did you go into that building hunting your ex with intent to kill him?"

"Of course not." Sophie met Chang's gaze, her eyes wide and guileless. "I merely wanted to ascertain Assan's presence in the building so that I could call the 'proper authorities,' as you have described them. In fact, I did talk over the situation with a detective on the case, and according to Sergeant Lei Texeira, the clue I had was too thin to submit to anyone, given the gallery owner's history with Maui Police Department."

Chang flipped to the crime scene photos and pushed them over to Sophie and Bennie Fernandez. Sophie made herself look, her expression neutral. Assan Ang lay on his back in a pool of blood. The gash in his neck was a gruesome smile.

"Assan Ang was unarmed. His throat was cut from behind. Tell me how this brutal killing is self-defense."

Sophie described the series of events. "Assan was not unarmed. He was armed with a phone that showed my friend, Sergeant

Texeira, who I mentioned before, being held prisoner. Bound and gagged. Tortured by him, with the push of a button."

"You have statements from responding officers and Sergeant Texeira backing all this up," Fernandez chimed in. "You're trying to turn this into a witch hunt."

"No such thing. I'm merely attempting to determine if less than deadly force might have been enough to restrain Assan Ang." Chang's chill dark gaze fastened on Sophie. "Tell me again why you killed him."

Sophie licked dry lips and swallowed. Herein lay the crux of the matter. "I knew this man intimately. I heard the inflection of Assan's voice when he said to me, 'She's dead. You brought this on her. I'll never tell you where she is,' and he cut off Lei's air with a push of a button. I knew in that moment that Assan had nothing but contempt for me. Even when I held a knife to his throat to bargain for my friend's life, he didn't take me seriously. I had lived through his tortures, punishments, and mental games for five years. I could not give in or Lei and I were both dead. If I took him out then, there was a chance I could find where he'd hidden her before she smothered."

"But you could have tied him, then searched him." Chang pointed to the photo documenting patterns in the congealing blood around the body, the dark fluid soaking the front of the man's clothing. "Evidence at the scene suggests you searched him twice."

"And that is in my original statement, one I'm sure that's been backed up by Jake Dunn. My partner helped me search him the second time, when I found the key to the room where Assan intended to keep me captive."

"There is no evidence he planned to..."

"Respectfully, Mr. District Attorney, I disagree." Sophie glared at Chang. "Assan Ang used the 'safe room' in our apartment in Hong Kong to keep me in complete darkness. For days. In between episodes of sexual and other torture. That chamber that we found was outfitted much as that room in our apartment had been."

Bennie Fernandez cleared his throat and held up a hand. "Ms.

Ang is clearly a victim of battered woman syndrome. Battered woman syndrome is now recognized in legislation by many states and is considered when defending battered wives who kill or injure their abusive spouses."

Sophie frowned at Fernandez, feeling defensive. She didn't have a "syndrome." She had not only escaped—she'd overcome that monster's grip and given him better than he deserved with a quick death!

Fernandez held up his hand again toward Chang, who'd opened his mouth in rebuttal. "BWS is an indication of the defendant's state of mind and in court, will be considered a mitigating circumstance. A Hawaii court will likely consider that as a BWS woman, Ms. Ang felt that she was justified in attacking her abuser, and that she was in reasonable fear of imminent danger due to her condition and her experiences with the abuser."

"Are you a psychologist, Mr. Fernandez?" Chang asked. "Has Ms. Ang been diagnosed with this supposed condition?"

Sophie squeezed her hands together in her lap, restraining herself from speaking. *"Let him defend you; that's what he's there for,"* Marcella's voice said in her head.

"A mere technicality," Fernandez said. "If you move ahead with these charges, you may count on expert witnesses and a psychological assessment to bolster the argument."

Chang's phone chimed, and he glanced down at it. "I have to take this." The man gestured for the recording equipment to be turned off and exited the room.

Fernandez turned to Sophie.

Sophie's cheeks felt hot and her eyes dry. Her pulse was hammering.

Anger. That's what she felt. Anger! She had done what needed to be done to rid the world of a sadistic killer. These men were patronizing her: minimizing her judgment call in the moment, turning her necessary dispatch of Assan Ang into the knee-jerk act of a helpless, beaten woman.

"Don't say it," Fernandez held up a hand toward her, much as he had done toward Chang. "We don't know what's still recording, who's still watching."

"I do not like this line of defense," Sophie persisted.

"I don't care, my dear. It is both appropriate and indicated in your situation."

Sophie's gaze shifted to the mirrored wall behind Fernandez. She rolled her lips between her teeth and bit down on them to silence herself. She couldn't wait to get out of there and "kick the shit out of something," as Jake would say.

Chang returned. His face had gone sallow with stress and there were beads of sweat on his upper lip. "This deposition is adjourned. You will be informed if further statements need to be taken."

"My client has work to return to," Fernandez said. "This is most inconvenient."

"Your client needs to stay available until we make a determination in these proceedings," Chang said, and exited again.

Fernandez stood, gestured toward the door in a courtly way. "After you."

Sophie went to the door, opened it, and gestured to Fernandez while holding it open. "No, sir. After *you.*"

Out in the hall, Fernandez touched her arm. "A case is all about perception."

"What about truth?" Sophie turned to the cherubic little man.

"Truth is perception. There are facts, and then there is how those facts are presented." Fernandez tugged down his wrinkled cotton jacket. "You heard the man. Stay available for a return interview."

Sophie glanced at the clock. "I have somewhere to be. Thank you for your efforts, Mr. Fernandez."

"Bennie, please. Call me Bennie," Fernandez called after Sophie, but she didn't look back, heading for the front of the building as fast as she could without running. She couldn't wait to get away from both lawyers.

CHAPTER FORTY-ONE

ALIKA FELT underdressed in his sleeveless black Fight Club tee shirt and jeans as he pushed open a large brass-and-glass door to the swanky Honua Pub in downtown Honolulu, the address Frank Smithson had texted him.

"Beer garden, my ass," Alika muttered as he stepped into a dim interior, cool with air-conditioning and gleaming with expensive leather and wood. A pretty hostess in a fitted black dress raised her brows in inquiry as he approached the stand. "I'm here to meet Frank Smithson."

"Oh, the ambassador is already here. Your other party has already arrived, too. Follow me."

Other party? Alika's heart rate spiked. Maybe Sophie was already here, done with her deposition. He followed the hostess through the dignified restaurant and bar to a private area in the back.

Frank Smithson stood as Alika entered, and so did another man. This guy was large and ripped, with cold gray eyes, and his buzz-cut hair and crisp movements spoke military.

"Alika, I want you to meet Jake Dunn, Sophie's work partner at Security Solutions. Jake, this is Alika Wolcott. He coached Sophie's fighting for years."

"Good to meet you." Dunn wrung Alika's hand, his tone curt.

"Likewise." Alika gave back as good as he got, crunching Dunn's bones in his grip. What a prick! What was his problem?

The men sat. Beers and menus arrived. Alika avoided Dunn's steady stare, taking in the room's elegant appointments. "I should've known that when an ambassador invites you to a pub, a suit jacket is in order."

"Hardly." Frank had a mellow bass laugh. "But you are right. The Honua Pub is a bit old-fashioned. I wasn't expecting Jake, but Sophie invited him. And I don't know either of you well. Tell me who you are and what you do." His dark brown gaze was level and piercing. "And how well you know my daughter."

Alika glanced over at Dunn. The other man's eyes shifted away. He flicked a finger at Alika. "You go first."

"Well, as you know, Frank, I'm a businessman. I met Sophie five years ago at my gym, Fight Club downtown. Began coaching her in MMA, and as you may be aware, she's very talented. Last year we went out a few times." Alika took a sip of his beer. "I got injured in a situation related to one of her cases and decided to go back to Kaua'i, where most of my construction business is based, and let things cool off."

"Sophie said you broke up," Frank said. "I know she missed you when she got injured."

"We agreed to stop seeing each other, yes, mainly due to geography and unfinished business with her ex. And I'm sorry I wasn't there for her through her injury." His throat had gone dry, and Alika took another sip of beer. "I thought a clean break was best. But that could be changing. I'm open to a new start if she is."

Alika hadn't meant to declare himself like this, but as he met Dunn's gaze he felt the truth of his words. He wanted to be with Sophie, and he wasn't intimidated by the competition. Dunn narrowed his eyes, folding his arms over his chest so that they bulged. *Asshole.* Alika wasn't impressed. "Long distance doesn't work for me, though, so we'll see. I've got plenty going on with my main business right now. We are building a good-sized 'green' low-income housing project on Kaua'i that's keeping me there, and I've got my own chopper. That's why Marcella contacted me about finding Sophie in Kalalau and bringing her back for the deposition."

Jake Dunn interrupted, ignoring Alika as if he hadn't spoken. "Aren't you worried about Sophie leaving her job at Security Solutions and going off the grid?" He directed the question to Frank.

Frank eyed the younger man. "I know my daughter well enough to know I can't tell her much of anything. I've got my line drawn in the sand with her: she has to check in with me every three days. She tries to abide by that. But I would never be fool enough to try to tell her what to do."

Jake rolled his eyes. "You got that right. It's made being her partner tough sometimes."

"I can imagine. But what you can trust is that Sophie knows what she's doing, and can take care of herself. She survived Assan Ang, after all." Frank's mouth tightened grimly. "What she needs is people who believe in her and support her. Even when she goes off the rails, like it seems she's done now. She's just trying to find her way, and she will. I hope both of you will help her, not get in her way."

"I've known her too long to imagine I could tell her anything," Alika said. "But Dunn here seems to think otherwise. Dunn, want to fill me and the ambassador in on why?"

"Sophie is new to private security. I'm not." The muscle-bound prick went on to describe his career in Special Forces. He'd seen action everywhere from Fallujah to Bangkok, and he had been working in private security since he retired from the military. "Sophie is incredible. Great instincts, too many talents to count, off the charts with tech. But she's inexperienced in some ways—naïve. Doesn't have experience with undercover work, hasn't had time enough in the field. She's been injured a number of times since she left the FBI, and not small incidents, either. She's not alert enough to her surroundings. Misinterprets people. Has a tough time operating undercover in terms of playing a part. And all that…makes me worry." Dunn hid his emotion behind his beer stein, but Alika saw it.

This guy had it bad for her, and it wouldn't pay to underestimate him.

Dunn had the look of a dirty fighter.

CHAPTER FORTY-TWO

SOPHIE PUSHED through the doors of the Honua Pub, her father's favorite hangout, with Marcella in tow. The men, seated at a round corner table, rose to greet them. Sophie approached her father first, giving him a big hug.

He patted her shoulder. "How was the deposition, darling?"

"I survived."

"Sophie had Bennie Fernandez, nastiest little defense lawyer this side of the Rocky Mountains, in her corner," Marcella said. "It doesn't get any better than that. Hey, Jake. And Alika! Aren't you a sight for sore eyes. Looking good, my friend."

Marcella's poise and upbeat, flirtatious manner seemed to relax a tense atmosphere as Sophie turned from her father's embrace to give Jake a quick hug. "Good to see you, partner."

"You had us worried," Jake said. "Glad you're back in the land of the living."

"Speaking of that." Sophie turned to Alika. "Would you mind accompanying me to see Nakai in the hospital? I heard he's doing okay but I think a visit from familiar faces would be good for him."

Alika nodded. "Of course. That kid is attached to you, and unless they found some relatives of his over here, he's alone."

"The system hasn't forgotten him," Marcella said as they all took seats. "While Sophie was in giving her deposition, I took the liberty of calling our friend Lei on Maui to tap on some Child Welfare contacts on Kaua'i. She got the name of a really good foster care worker, and we're working on putting together a special group home placement so all the boys can stay together."

Alika grinned. "Perfect. I didn't want to just go in and take away the only home they had without anything to offer."

"Don't forget, those boys were ready to throw you in a hole and bury you," Sophie said.

"What? This story I've got to hear!" Jake exclaimed.

Sophie perused the menu as Alika explained how they'd moved the boulder and found a way down into the lava tube where the missing boy was trapped. "Sophie found her way down by falling in! Thankfully, it was a short drop. Of course, she took off by herself to find the boy while I was tying off a rope. Poor kid was trapped—had his leg crushed by a boulder. When I got back out to fetch the first responders to the site, I was confronted by five of the teens who the boy had been living with in a cave on the mountain. There's an adult with them everyone calls the Shepherd; the guy seems to be calling the shots, and there is some secret he wanted kept. So, the boys tried to shove me in the hole to shut me up."

"The Shepherd sets himself up as a father figure, but he sexually abuses the boys," Sophie said. "I talked to the man before we found Nakai, and he lied about what happened. He must have sent the boys to follow us. They seem to be thoroughly under his control."

"Yeah. Things got physical when the kids rushed me. I had to take a few of them down, and the disturbance caused the lip of the hole to collapse. One of the boys was caught in the cave-in that occurred. We kind of bonded getting him out from being buried alive." Sophie enjoyed the animation in Alika's face as he described the events. "Long story short, I was really happy to see Sophie come up out of that hole by the end."

"You two certainly had an adventure. Thank God it turned out all right. And that chopper of yours seems to be coming in handy," Frank said.

"That's Alika's chick magnet," Marcella said. Alika ducked his head in embarrassment, rubbing the back of his neck. Years ago, he'd dated Lei and taken her out on the helicopter, a story Lei had told Sophie before she knew of Sophie's interest in him. The memory gave Sophie a little twinge, as it always had. But Lei was well and truly married, and Alika seemed totally over her…or was he? She'd never been sure.

The group told stories of other places, other rescues. Jake had done some crazy things extracting kidnap victims in South America and, one time, airplane survivors in a crash in Lithuania. Before she knew it, time and the meal had passed.

Sophie glanced at Alika. "We should go. I want to see Nakai and tell him we're working on the foster home situation before visiting hours are over."

"We're finished here, anyway," Frank said, and paid the check over the rest of the table's protests.

They all stood. Marcella said goodbye, and Sophie and Alika headed for the exit. Jake hurried around the table to grasp Sophie by the arm. "Hey. Don't run off. I want to keep in touch."

Sophie let Alika go ahead to the doors at the restaurant and turned to Jake. "I'll give you my new number. But you won't be able to reach me out there, anyway."

"Humor me. And why are you going back to Kaua'i?"

"I'm not done out there in Kalalau. There's unfinished business with the Shepherd to attend to." Sophie took a pen from the hostess stand, grabbed Jake's hand and turned it over. She wrote the number of her latest burner cell phone on the inside of his forearm as he laughed.

"What is this? The nineteen-nineties?"

"My phone's dead right now." Gripping his wrist, Sophie's nostrils flared as she took in his familiar scent of lemony aftershave and man. His arm was thick and sinewy, but the veins crossing his wrist were tenderly blue and vulnerable. She had a ridiculous urge to kiss that nexus of veins.

She paused, the pen denting his skin. *She didn't want to move away just yet.*

"Sophie," Jake whispered. She felt that whisper on the back of her neck, and all the way down to her toes. If she looked up, she would see what was in his eyes, so she didn't look up. *She couldn't.* She dropped his wrist like it burned her, and in a way, it did.

"I'll be in touch, Jake."

She hurried through the doors without looking back.

HER FATHER DROVE them to the hospital in his big Lincoln Continental. She kissed Frank goodbye at the drop-off zone. "I'll take a ride-share back to the apartment and spend this evening with you, Dad."

"That better be a promise."

Alika said goodbye to her father as well, and they entered the children's hospital's busy lobby. Getting directions, Sophie was relieved that she and Alika were on the list admitted to see Nakai.

In the elevator, Alika reached for her hand as they ascended to Nakai's wing. "Come here."

Sophie was tired, her emotions battered by the hostile hours in the deposition. Ever-present sadness waited to pounce: there were men who loved her, and whom she loved, too—*and yet she was alone.* "And you always will be," the depression's poisonous voice whispered. "You ruin everything you touch."

Sophie let Alika draw her into his arms so that she leaned against him, their bodies aligned, her back to his front, his arms crossed over her waist, her hands holding them in front of her. He felt like a warm solid wall. Sophie closed her eyes to savor the feeling of support.

She vividly remembered riding down the elevator from her father's apartment with Alika in just this pose over a year ago, and the feeling of rightness and comfort that it had brought her then, too.

But a lot had happened since, including her relationship with Connor. It was wrong to indulge in his touch, no matter how badly she craved it. She couldn't bear to hurt either of them again, and she didn't trust herself any more. She'd just been struggling with the same sorts of impulses with Jake! *She was a mess.*

Sophie moved away and stood on the other side of the elevator, watching the numbers change over the door.

CHAPTER FORTY-THREE

NAKAI SAT PROPPED up in the hospital bed. He spooned a third helping of bright red Jell-O rapidly into his mouth.

"Slow down, boy. You'll give yourself a tummy ache." Mrs. Feliciano, the social worker from child welfare, was a short, apple-shaped woman wearing a denim muumuu. Her skinny legs were dressed in leggings patterned with mangoes. The orange of the mangoes hurt his eyes.

The doctor who had checked Nakai out said there was no medical reason for his constant sense of being overwhelmed whenever he opened his eyes. He had been underground for four days, and his system had adapted to less stimulation. "You should be fine in time," The doctor said. But until then, Nakai insisted they keep the room's lights off.

"I brought you a pair of sunglasses." Mrs. Feliciano handed Nakai a pair of cool aviators. Nakai put them on, looking around. "Thanks."

Talking kind of hurt, too. Sounds seemed too loud as well as colors too bright.

"Some visitors are on their way." Mrs. Feliciano had taken charge of him from the moment the helicopter brought him into the hospital. Since his mother could not be found, nor any other relatives located, he was temporarily a ward of the state. He'd have worried about what that meant, but Mrs. Feliciano took her duties very seriously.

Nakai found her bossiness comforting. She treated him like a mom who took her "mom job" seriously.

Unlike his real mom. Enola didn't care.

His mind shied away from that thought. Mom did the best she could. Her addiction was "a disease" according to one of his school counselors.

"Who's coming to see me? Is it Mom?"

"They still haven't located your mother, Nakai. Your visitors are that woman, Sandy Mason, who rescued you, and her friend, Alika Wolcott."

Nakai grinned and bounced a little, which jarred his leg. *That hurt.* He put his tray aside. "Can I comb my hair?"

"Of course. You want to look your best." Mrs. Feliciano cleared his tray and took a comb, toothbrush, and toothpaste out of the travel kit she'd brought for him. "They won't believe how good you're looking."

Nakai did feel a lot better, even though his leg was immobilized in a traction sling. He had had a bedside tub shower and sponge bath once he was settled in, and after so many days of filth, it had taken both Mrs. Feliciano and a nurse's aide a good hour to scrub off all the grime.

"What's going to happen to me?" Nakai asked, trying to keep the quiver out of his voice as he tugged the comb through his hair.

Mrs. Feliciano patted his arm and opened her mouth to speak, but a light tap on the door interrupted them.

"Come in!" the social worker called. The door opened to reveal the woman Nakai had barely been able to make out in the dark.

Sandy Mason was taller than he'd realized, only a few inches shorter than the Hawaiian man named Alika who had helped them. Sophie had long legs and hair cut short like a man's, and she was way prettier than he had imagined. Her face broke into a big smile at the sight of him, and she came over and bent down to give him a hug. She smelled of coconut oil and good things.

Mrs. Feliciano introduced herself as Alika took the chair on one side of his bed and Sandy the other. Sandy held his hand as she had down in the tunnel. She felt like land in the ocean, a fixed point he could hang onto.

Mrs. Feliciano told about the details of the surgery that had been done to fix his leg, and the likely amount of time needed for him to recover: close to a month.

"But I'll be up and on crutches way sooner than that," Nakai said. "And I don't want to return to Kalalau. I want to go back to school." So many things had become clearer to him in the darkness. Even though he was a kid, he wasn't totally helpless.

"You don't have to go back to Kalalau." Sandy squeezed his fingers, and he squeezed back. "We're working on a situation so that you and the other boys can all be together."

This should have made him feel good, but Nakai hadn't been with the lost boys long enough to really bond with them, and he had broken code by telling what the Shepherd was doing to him.

Nakai looked down, pleating the white sheet. Even though his hands had been scrubbed, there was still dirt under his nails from days of digging for worms. Seeing the dirt reminded him how strong he was, that he could survive, and that he needed to speak up for what he wanted.

"I don't want to live with the other boys. I just want a family to stay with." He looked up and met Mrs. Feliciano's eyes. "I would like to stay with Mrs. Feliciano and her family."

Alika cleared his throat. "I totally get that, man. You want to be with someone familiar."

"It's not just that. The boys will be angry with me for telling about the Shepherd, and I know how things work. I will have to give more testimony for him to get busted. They will want to kill me."

Nakai saw a look pass between Sophie and Alika. Yes, there were things they weren't telling him that involved the boys.

Mrs. Feliciano shook her head. "I'm a social worker, Nakai, not a foster parent."

"Please." He turned to her. He didn't know what to say, so just gave her his best puppy-dog eyes. "I won't be any trouble. I will follow all of your rules. I'm good at chores, and I can even cook."

A long moment passed as Mrs. Feliciano considered him. Suddenly, she slapped her mango-covered thighs abruptly, standing up from the plastic chair she had been seated on. "All right. I will make some phone calls." She turned, opened the door, and left.

Sandy's big brown eyes widened in surprise even as Alika broke into a huge grin and high-fived Nakai. "Way to tug on those heart-strings, kid. And I agree with you that being with the other boys is probably not the right situation."

"We're going back to Kalalau to finish up the investigation into the Shepherd and make sure the investigators have all the information," Sandy said. "We will look for your mother, too. Is there any message you want to give her if we find her?"

Nakai let go of Sandy's hand and pleated the sheet, thinking about his mom. "Tell her I love her, but I don't want to live with her anymore. And thank her for finding you and getting you to find me." Nakai picked up a pair of controllers from the side table, holding them up. "Either of you two know how to play Super Mario Brothers?"

CHAPTER FORTY-FOUR

B<small>ACK AT HER</small> father's apartment, Sophie sat in her quiet bedroom, blackout drapes drawn, headphones filled with classical music, poised in front of the keyboard.

She looked down at her hands. Her fingers were still long and golden brown, but now marred by scratches. Her nails were short and broken, and a rim of dirt lingered under her thumbnail. Crawling through that blinding dark on her hands and knees had "worked them over" as Marcella would say. But how had it become so unfamiliar so quickly to sit in front of a computer? So much had changed—not that long ago, being "wired in" to her computers had been her norm.

Sophie opened the DAVID program. She typed in all the information she had on the Shepherd, which wasn't much, and set the program to searching for more information. A few minutes later, DAVID produced a mug shot matching the man she'd met in the cave—real name Barton Kuiaha. He'd been convicted in 1998 of molestation of a minor during his job as a youth correctional officer. After being fired and serving six months of probation and counseling, he'd disappeared. "Not even a tax return filed," Sophie muttered.

DAVID could only work with law enforcement and public data

already entered; if Barton Kuiaha had gone "off the grid" and had no other information available, he was invisible to the program.

Sophie glanced over at the squat black external hard drive containing the Ghost software. *The time had come to break open the beast.* The Ghost could penetrate areas she'd never programmed DAVID to go to find this man.

Sophie forced her fingers to type in the password Connor had constructed.

The screen bloomed open to the Ghost program's search parameters. She typed in the Shepherd's physical height, approximate weight, age, and general description. She drop-filled in the "nickname and moniker" section with "Shepherd."

She turned away to pet Ginger while the program was searching. "Hey girl. You treat my dad okay while I was gone?" Ginger dropped to the ground and rolled on Sophie's feet in reply, exposing her belly for a toe rub. Sophie obliged.

Sophie was too wound up to relax. She couldn't stop thinking of Nakai, and his heartfelt appeal to Mrs. Feliciano.

If only she could be the one giving that boy a place to live—but the barren Mary Watson apartment hardly qualified as a home.

Sophie sighed and glanced up at the Ghost program to see what had loaded. She jerked in surprise. A chat window marked *The Ghost* had appeared.

"I see you are giving the program a try, Sophie."

Connor was reaching out to her through the program. Sophie felt her whole body flush with feelings she couldn't identify.

Of course, Connor would have a "call home" beacon built into the Ghost program that pinged him whenever it was activated. He might even have a Remote Access Trojan embedded in the software that could take over her webcam or computer.

In opening the Ghost program, she opened herself to *him*.

Sophie spun to the keyboard and tried to shut it down. The program resisted, popping open multiple chat windows against her attempts.

The dialogue box lit up again. *"I promise I am not spying on you. I haven't even run a trace to identify where you are, though of course you know I could do that. I'm trying to be respectful. I just wanted to see if I could help with whatever you're working on."*

Sophie frowned, and leaned forward as she typed rapidly. *"That's how you always begin. By being polite and respectful, and then becoming indispensable."*

"So, I'm indispensable?"

Sophie sucked her bottom lip between her teeth, hating that she'd slipped up and given him an opening. *"You want to be. You want me in your power, in your debt, and it's not going to happen. I fell for your mind games one time, and grieved over what I thought was your body. Never again."*

"I'm sorry, Sophie. I hated to do that to you. To us. Please let me make it up to you."

"There is nothing that you could do that will make up for that, in this or any universe. And if you were really being respectful, you would leave me alone."

"I have been helping you. You won't be bothered by that DA any longer. Any charges against you for Assan Ang's death will be dropped."

Sophie's fingers froze over the keyboard. She remembered the phone call the DA had received, and the sight of his sweating, pale face before he abruptly ended her deposition.

"What did you do?"

"Nothing that need concern you. But let's just say, DA Chang is a candidate for a little Ghost treatment. He's not as clean as he appears."

"I don't need or want your help with Chang, or anything else. I don't want to see you, hear from you, or have my life played with by you. Leave me alone. I cannot be clearer than that." Heat flushed Sophie's body.

"As you wish."

The chat box disappeared, and the Ghost program shut down. A photo of a fresh, dew-spattered red rose appeared on the screen, and dissolved in a flurry of tiny hearts.

"Ridiculous," Sophie muttered. She groped for the American word. "Corny."

But as she unplugged the Ghost's external hard drive and ran a diagnostic virus and malware removal program to make sure her rig was clear of any trace of the Ghost, she fought a warm tingly feeling.

Connor was out there, somewhere, watching over her.

CHAPTER FORTY-FIVE

ALIKA GLANCED OVER AT SOPHIE. Her full curved lips were set in a firm line, her eyes forward. He could stare at her profile all day, damn it, even with her helmet on. He reached over to tug at her four-point seat harness, making sure it was secure as he prepped the Dragonfly for departure to Kalalau. Ginger whined from the back of the chopper, where she was secured with a leash.

Sophie turned to reassure the dog. "It's okay, girl."

Alika wasn't sure it was okay. They were flying to Kaua'i and meeting with a couple of detectives before taking them to the remote valley to deal with the Shepherd and the boys out there. "I don't think you should lie to the cops," he said. "You should tell them you're Sophie Ang."

Sophie turned to look at him, those big brown eyes wide, her brows raised. That wicked gunshot scar just made her face more interesting. "I don't want to alert them in case the situation with my ex becomes an issue. I'm not supposed to leave the island."

"Then you shouldn't leave the island. Let me handle it. I can go to Kaua'i, meet the detectives, show them the location. You don't need to put yourself out there right now."

Sophie's mouth tightened into a mulish line he remembered from her fighting days. That line signaled that she'd just doubled down on her position, whatever it was. "You don't understand."

"I guess I don't. Don't you trust me to be able to get the boys the help they need?"

"And what if it's not help they need? What if it's something stronger? You've already covered up for them once."

"Ah. So then, you don't trust me."

Their gazes clashed.

Sophie took off her helmet. Alika did the same.

Sophie drew a breath, meeting his eyes. "It's not that I don't trust you. It's that I know how investigations work. A witness reporting something automatically becomes involved, because there are many reasons people report things, not all of them altruistic. Questions will be raised about...how you got involved. They will dig into your past, and I know you've dealt with Jenkins before because Lei told me you came under investigation one time. They will want to interview 'Sandy Mason' and find out how I located Nakai."

"I know Lei was the one to reach out to Jenkins and get the group home set up. There's no way she would go along with lying to her former partner," Alika said. Lei's integrity was bone-deep and had been one of the things he'd liked most about the woman he'd dated so long ago.

"You're right, she wouldn't ever lie to him." Sophie's mouth twisted ruefully. "I'll have to take a chance and hope that they don't look into Sandy Mason too closely. There's no reason they should. I just need to see this situation through."

"If you insist." Alika put on his helmet, ending the discussion. Sophie put on hers, tightening the chin strap as Alika suppressed the roiling of his gut by doing the pre-flight check. His mind ticked back over the last day.

He'd returned to Fight Club after their visit with Nakai and had spent the night at Chewy's house. Coming to Oahu had reminded him that he had a life he'd worked hard to build on this island, and friends he could count on.

Even if Sophie didn't end up being one of them.

He might not see her again after today. Beyond the one kiss they'd shared, she'd given him no reason to hope there was going to be anything more.

"Are you going to want to stay in Kalalau after we deal with the Shepherd?" Alika asked, his finger poised above the Start button on the control panel.

Sophie frowned, a slight scrunch of her smooth forehead. "I don't know. I'm keeping all my options open."

"How nice for you. Some of us have actual jobs. Commitments." Alika was unable to suppress a flash of temper. "I've taken off a lot of time to help you out, and flying this bird isn't cheap, either."

Sophie turned to him, eyes wide. "I can pay you."

"I don't want your money." He gazed at her a long moment, trying to read her smooth, neutral face. Trying not to be insulted—he'd opened that door himself. He hid the bruised feeling in his chest with a brusque nod. "But perhaps that would be best. I'll give you a total for the chopper's gas, at least."

He pushed the Start button. The blades overhead began to whirl and vibration shook the frame as the Dragonfly came to life.

Sophie put her hand on his arm. Her voice, tinny through the comm unit built into the helmet, filled his ear. "Thank you."

He didn't want her thanks. He didn't want her money, either. He wanted *her*.

Alika shook her hand off his arm and grasped the collective.

The sound and vibration killed any further angst, and Alika relished the power beneath his hands as he lifted the Dragonfly into the still, cool morning air over Honolulu. They rose, and swept off the top of the building. He heard Sophie's breathless gasp as Honolulu, backlit by morning just beginning to rise over the mountains, swooped out below, and the ocean, glittering like blue foil, spread before them.

Alika loved flying in the early morning before the wind came up to mar the surface of the water and make the ride rough. He set his heading and flew the chopper at max rpms toward Kaua'i.

Once underway, he sneaked a glance at Sophie.

She had pressed her face to the window and was scanning the cobalt water below as they arrowed swiftly over it, flying low.

"Look!" Her big dark eyes were bright with excitement through the helmet as she pointed to a whale cow and calf, rising to the surface beneath them.

Alika smiled and gave a thumbs-up. *Whales never got old.* He pointed to a pod of dolphins as they approached Kaua'i, and the great batlike shape of a manta ray moving along just under the surface of the water.

They eventually set down at the Kaua'i Police Department's helipad just behind the new, urban-ugly KPD building outside Kapa'a. Lei Texeira's ex-partner, Jack Jenkins, was meeting them with another detective.

Alika took off his helmet and turned to Sophie as she shook out her short hair and set her helmet aside, unclipping the harness. "Last chance to bail. You sure you want to go through with this? We are both just civilians in the situation."

Sophie regarded him steadily. "That's right. That's all we both are. But we are talented, useful civilians." She winked, and that startled a laugh out of him.

"All right, have it your way."

They got out of the chopper and walked over to meet Jack Jenkins, who'd exited the building with a partner. Lei had called the five-ten, stocky, muscular young man with his gelled blond hair "J-Boy."

"Good to see you again, Alika," Jenkins's handshake was firm. "And this must be Sandy, the hiker who uncovered all of this." The detective's gaze on Sophie was assessing.

"Hello." Sophie extended her hand. "I set out to have an adventure on Kaua'i, and it's really been one."

"My partner, Paul Nae'ole." Jenkins introduced a thickset Hawaiian man who had joined them.

Alika recognized the man from paddling. "You with Nawiliwili Canoe Club?" They exchanged pleasantries, and Jenkins jerked his head toward the aircraft.

"So, we just need you to take us to the area where the Shepherd and those boys are camping. We'll take the investigation from there."

"When we visited him in the hospital, the boy we rescued, Nakai, reiterated his accusations about the Shepherd. And he's anxious about his mother, and being made to share a foster home with the other boys. He's worried they will hate him for disclosing the abuse," Sophie said.

"All in good time." Jenkins's cop face was unreadable. "Everyone is innocent until proven guilty."

Sophie tightened her lips but said nothing. Alika cleared his throat. "Let me speak to your pilot and share my flight plan."

IT WASN'T long before they were in the air again after the Dragon-fly's tank was topped off. Sweeping around the magnificent crags and corrugated depths of Kauai's Na Pali cliffs was challenging, and even with all that was going on, Alika enjoyed the skill of keeping the craft steady and straight as he led the police chopper along the route they'd established, and then set the bird down in the now-familiar meadow near the trail.

"We need you to show us where the cave is, but we will make the approach," Jenkins told Sophie, when they were all out of the craft and on the ground. "Stay back until we signal you."

Sophie's lips tightened again, but she nodded. Alika glanced at the Kevlar vests the two cops wore, their sidearms at the ready. Once again, they left Ginger, this time tied to the strut of the Dragonfly. She whined fretfully but didn't offer any further resistance as the group set off up the trail.

"We plan to assess the situation when we go in," Jenkins said. "We have a foster situation set up, but these things always go better if we build trust first."

"I don't see that happening," Sophie said. "The boys were after Nakai and were a part of causing the lava tube to collapse, trapping us in there. They attacked Alika."

"What?" The two cops came to a halt and looked back at him.

Alika sighed, shaking his head. "I didn't want to get them in trouble if it wasn't necessary. They're just brainwashed, confused kids."

"Brainwashed, confused kids prepared to commit murder to cover up an accusation against their leader," Sophie said, her tone hard. "These investigators need all the facts going in."

"We definitely needed to know this. We should expect resistance. Wish you'd told us this back at KPD headquarters," Nae'ole said.

Alika tried not to tense up as the cops grilled him about the attack and how it had resolved.

"We would have brought additional backup. What weapons do these boys have?" Jenkins asked. Sophie described them in detail. Jenkins frowned. "What did you say your background was?" Clearly her knowledgeability was drawing their attention.

"Former FBI agent. I used to work in private security."

They seemed to accept this, though Jenkins wore a puzzled frown.

"Well, we'll go in, get a temperature check and see what we see," Nae'ole said. "You two stay well back until we signal you."

Sophie led them to a hidden trail off the main track toward the back of the valley. They eventually ended up at a waterfall gushing in a generous spray that hid the cave entrance.

"It's through there." Sophie pointed to a dark slit of opening masked by the path of the water.

Alika had brought up the rear of their small cavalcade, and he and Sophie slipped behind the sheltering bole of a *kukui* nut tree as the two detectives proceeded with caution, keeping behind cover as they approached the dark slit near the cascade.

"I don't like this," Sophie whispered. Before Alika could stop her, she darted after the men and ducked into the shadow cast by the waterfall.

CHAPTER FORTY-SIX

Sᴏᴘʜɪᴇ ʜᴇʟᴅ onto the rocky edge of the cave's opening, slick beneath her fingers, cold and damp with overspray. The roar of the cataract drowned out any sounds from inside the cavern as she inched forward, wishing for the familiar weight of her Glock.

She glanced back.

Alika gestured frantically for her to return. She shook her head, a short movement, and slipped around the curve of stone into the darkness beyond.

Murky dim dropped over her, enfolding her in the familiar cloak of darkness. Letting her eyes adjust, Sophie settled into stillness behind a sheltering rock protrusion. She could hope that the uneven, flickering light of the small fire in the center of the room barely glazed her golden-brown skin.

The silhouettes of Nae'ole and Jenkins briefly blocked the fire's glow, and she couldn't make out the shape of their drawn weapons but knew they'd have them out. She scanned the large expanse of the cavern, but saw no one else. The only other light was the steady bluish glow of the LED lantern she had seen in the Shepherd's tent, and the men were headed for it.

Sophie trotted on light feet in their wake, hoping to remain undetected so that they didn't send her back out, or worse, shoot her.

The detectives took up a cover position behind a large metal barrel near the tent. "Come out! Kaua'i Police Department!" Jenkins's voice echoed in the enclosed space.

No reply.

Sophie's hands curled into fists and her nails dug into her palms. She uncurled them, longing for her weapon, but she'd decided when she first set out not to complicate her travels with a gun.

"Cover me," Jenkins said to his partner, and trotted forward to the little tent. Sophie heard the sound of the zipper and a quick intake of breath. "We have a body."

"Jenkins. Nae'ole." It was time to identify herself. Sophie stepped forward, her open hands up, advancing slowly so that the men could recognize her. "It's me, Sandy. Maybe I can help. I have met the Shepherd, and the boys."

"What the hell? Get back outside." Nae'ole grabbed Sophie's arm in a biting grip. "You're lucky we didn't shoot you!"

This was what she got for being nothing but a civilian, not even a hired contractor with a security job. "I can save time. Maybe identify the body for you."

Jenkins addressed Nae'ole from the door of the tent. "Let her get a look. She's right; it could speed things up."

Nae'ole glared and kept his weapon on her, but allowed Sophie to approach the tent's opening. They both peered in over Jenkins's kneeling form.

A man lay face down. He was dressed in the clothing Sophie remembered: a pair of dingy sweat pants and a *kihei* robe of tapa cloth, tied at one shoulder. What had once been a full head of flowing, silver hair was now a pulpy red mess.

"I can't be sure without seeing his face, but the height, build, and clothing are consistent with the man referred to as the Shepherd. I did an online search the other night and found a name to match his description: Barton Kuiaha. He's a former youth correctional officer who was fired for child molesting back in 1998."

Jenkins looked up at her, his square, good-natured face alert, his eyes narrowed. "You talk like a cop."

"I told you I was former FBI." Sophie kept her neutral expression in place that hid her feelings, thoughts, or needs. "And very recently, in private security." *She was going to be brought in for questioning more closely, no doubt about it.* Unless she could get away, her Sandy Mason identity was going to be blown.

"I can't get a signal to call for backup and the CSI team," Nae'ole said, his voice tight with tension as he worked his phone one-handed. "I don't like this."

"I don't think there's any signal outside either. We'll have to call from the chopper's radio." Jenkins stood up. "Nae'ole, stay here and secure the scene. Cover this woman while I check the cave for any other witnesses."

Sophie had become "this woman."

Nae'ole gave a hard nod. He held his weapon leveled at Sophie's midsection as Jenkins moved off into the dark, flicking on a small, high-powered flashlight and calling out an identification to anyone who might still be hiding in the shadows. "Kauai Police Department! Come out, we need to speak with you!"

He wouldn't find anyone—the boys would have fled. Sophie felt sure of it.

Sophie dropped to her haunches, examining the body from her vantage point in the tent's doorway. The blood pool was still bright and glossy; the coppery smell almost burned her nostrils. "He hasn't been dead long. There's the murder weapon." She pointed to a round rock about the size of a grapefruit, hidden from immediate view by the mattress. One side of it was dark with blood and matted silver hairs.

"You have no business here." Nae'ole grabbed Sophie's arm and pulled her out of the doorway. "Get over against the wall."

She rose to her feet as gracefully as she could. "I was just trying to help. I'm the one who found these boys, remember."

"Get over by the wall." Nae'ole just waved her away.

Sophie walked to the far wall, closest to the cave's exit. She turned back and watched the tableau of Nae'ole going into the tent to make a visual exam of the body while Jenkins continued his circuit around the huge cave.

This was her chance.

If she was brought in by KPD, her cover would be blown and District Attorney Chang might have the fuel he needed to lock her up for Assan's killing.

Sophie sidled toward the cave's entrance. Neither man so much as looked her way. She was out and into the blinding sun in seconds.

CHAPTER FORTY-SEVEN

MARCELLA LOOKED around the all-purpose conference room table in the FBI's team planning room. A bank of bulletproof windows faced the ocean. An embossed United States seal decorated with gold leaf marked the far wall and flags occupied one corner, while white-boards covered the rest of the space. Special Agent in Charge Ben Waxman, tech agent Joe Bateman, Lei's ex-partner Ken Yamada, and her own partner Matt Rogers looked back at Marcella.

Marcella tapped the file she'd set on the table in front of her. "I'm coming up dry on the trail of the Ghost cyber vigilante. I can't get any actionable intel on him. I have been trying to find proof of a shared identity between Todd Remarkian, recent bombing victim, and Sheldon Hamilton, CEO of Security Solutions. I thought I had found it when I uncovered the duplicate apartment in the Pendragon Arches building. But the CSI team found no DNA in either apartment matching Hamilton, or the body, identified as Todd Remarkian by dental records, that was found on the premises after the bombing. Sophie told me they were one and the same. Unfortunately, I can't prove that, let alone that Sheldon Hamilton is the Ghost."

"You sent me all this in your report the other day. Does anyone else have any leads?" Waxman's steel-blue gaze swept the room as he made notes on a slim laptop. A stack of files beside him gave a hint of things to come.

"I've been tracking Sheldon Hamilton's whereabouts," Yamada said, smoothing the lapels of his immaculate gray suit jacket, his handsome face serious. "As you all know, Sophie implicated Hamilton as the current identity behind the Ghost. Hamilton was staying at a suite at the Four Seasons and has since checked out. A Security Solutions SUV took him to the airport, where he took a private contracted jet to an undisclosed location. Without a warrant for the information, I couldn't get a flight plan—but if I were hazarding a guess, I'd say Hamilton went to Hong Kong. The company has an increasing footprint there."

"Security Solutions has been putting up every kind of firewall and security block they can to keep us out of their computers and personnel and other files," Bateman chimed in. Over the course of the investigation thus far, Marcella had come to respect the doughy young tech agent's way around a computer. He didn't have Sophie's genius; but then no one did. *Except, perhaps, the Ghost....*

Waxman steepled his fingers. "All right. Enough. This is now one of those back-burner investigations. Someday, sometime, the Ghost will slip up and tip his hand. And when he does, we will be waiting to scoop him up. But for now, we have a slew of new, real cases to dig our teeth into." Waxman reached over to the pile of folders. "These have come in in the last twenty-four hours. Keep your eyes, ears, and Internet browsers open for information about the Ghost; but for now, we have some alleged child pornographers, bomb makers, money launderers, and possible terrorists to bust."

Marcella and Matt Rogers received their stack of new cases, and after status updates, headed back to their office.

Matt bumped her with his sturdy shoulder. "You're awfully quiet today, partner." Rogers was ex-military, with the buzz-cut hair and precision work ethic to match. A deeply committed family man, Rogers always reminded Marcella that the job was just a job. She bumped him back.

"Thinking about Sophie. Missing her in our meetings, and after work, too." She'd had to loop Rogers in on what had happened between Sophie and the Ghost. She still wanted to nail that jerk for breaking her friend's heart, if nothing else. Sophie's latest romantic crash-and-burn hopefully wouldn't sour her love life forever. Sophie had choices with men, any of whom would have been better for her than the Ghost had been. Marcella's bet was on Jake in the long run. That guy was nothing if not persistent—and attractive.

"Sophie's tough as an old boot and twice as good at stompin'," Rogers said. He enjoyed letting his Texas twang out on occasion. "She'll land on her feet."

"You're over-fond of clichés, Mattie ol' pal." Marcella leaned into her partner for just a second. It was good to be surrounded by friends, and Sophie had chosen a lonely path. "I hope you're right about that."

The phone on her belt buzzed, and Marcella checked it. She turned to Rogers with wide eyes. "I have to take this. It's District Attorney Chang."

CHAPTER FORTY-EIGHT

ALIKA CURSED and his heart rate spiked as Sophie ran toward him from the mouth of the cave, her eyes wild. She flung her arms around him in a hug. Her skin was clammy with sweat and the chill cool spray from the waterfall as he held her close. "Are you okay? What the hell's going on?"

"I have to go." Sophie tore herself loose and turned to run down the path.

Alika followed at a jog. "And I repeat, what the hell's going on?"

"There was a body in the cave. The Shepherd had his head bashed in."

"Tell me you're kidding." Alika speeded up, his heart thudding. He ducked around a clump of ferns, dodging a big black rock. "Where were the boys?"

"Nowhere to be found."

"Why are you running?"

"Because the detectives are going to take me in for questioning. My fake identity will be blown. I don't have another one."

"Crap, Sophie!" Alika shoved a guava branch out of the way irritably as he ran. The trail was overgrown, narrow, and hazardous. He had to keep his eyes on his feet way more than he wanted to, but he managed to catch up and grab her shoulder. "Stop a minute. Tell me what I'm getting into by following you right now."

"Oh." Sophie turned toward him. Damn but she was gorgeous, color in her cheeks, pulse beating in her neck, mouth parted as she breathed hard. "You have to tell them you tried to grab me but I got away."

"The hell I will. If I grab you, you won't get away." Alika grasped her biceps, pulled her close. "See?"

"I've taken you down before," Sophie said. "And I can do it again." But she had gone still in his arms. An electric charge arced between their bodies.

"And what if I want you to take me down?" Alika bent his head to hers.

The kiss ignited that spark between them. He couldn't get enough of her lithe, strong body in his arms, her sweet taste and hungry mouth, the tiny sounds she made as they twined around each other. He wanted her now, right now, cops on their trail or no. *How had he ever thought he was over her?*

Sophie wrenched back, and, with a quick upward twist of her arms, was free. "I have to go. I'm sorry for dragging you into this. I'll get Ginger out of the chopper and be gone by the time they're even out of the cave."

"How is this a good idea? They're bound to catch you, and you'll just look guilty of something for running. We both know you're not guilty of anything but being a softie where kids are concerned."

"I'm guilty of not being who I said I was, and that's enough to make me a person of interest. If they can't find me, this will all blow over eventually and I'll surface when the coast is clear." Sophie touched his cheek. The ball of her thumb brushed his lips and made his blood surge. "It's hard to say goodbye."

"It always has been." Alika's voice came out harsher than he meant it to. He handed her the key to the chopper. "I tried to stop you, but you took the key from me. *Go.* This time you're the one running. That's some consolation."

Her eyes were stark. "I deserve that."

Sophie spun and ran. He watched her leap down the trail.

Alika's hands balled into fists at his sides. Being with Sophie was never going to be easy, but the truth was, he didn't really have a choice. It was her, or no one.

CHAPTER FORTY-NINE

ALIKA WAITED BY THE TREE, and soon Nae'ole emerged from the trail at a run. "Where's Sandy?"

"She blew past me in a rush. Said there was a body in the cave, that she needed to go to the chopper to call for help. I gave her the key." Alika had spent time thinking of what to say about Sophie's departure even though the feel and taste of Sophie still lingered on him.

"Shit. Yeah, there was a body. The guy they called the Shepherd had his head smashed in with a rock, and that woman knows way too much about it. We need to go back to our chopper to call. I can't get a signal here. Jenkins is staying with the body," Nae'ole said.

The two jogged back down the trail to the parked choppers. Nae'ole waved at their pilot. "Jimmy, get me the KPD chief on the radio."

Alika found his keys resting on the strut of the Dragonfly. "She's gone with her dog," he told Nae'ole.

The man cursed. "We'll have to track her down later for questioning."

Alika waited until all the response calls had been made for

backup, the medical examiner, and the crime scene techs. "Anything I can do to help?"

"You know this Sandy Mason. Why didn't you stop her?"

Alika didn't want to compound his lies. He shrugged. "I didn't know it was my job to stop her."

Nae'ole rolled his eyes in disgust. "Make yourself useful and come help me tape off the cave."

Alika followed him back and helped the detective rope off the cave's entrance with yellow crime scene tape. His body was tight with tension and worry for Sophie and for the boys. *Where had they gone? Which of them had killed their leader?*

He couldn't stop his worried thoughts, and soon the thrum of additional incoming helicopters filled the air. The choppers needed a different place to land, and eventually found a spot. Alika helped guide the incoming personnel to the cave. He stood back at last, feeling useless as the organized chaos unleashed by death unfolded around him in the peaceful setting.

Needing to relieve himself, Alika headed into a thick grove of kukui nut trees. He unzipped his fly behind a large boulder. The hairs rose on the back of his neck after a moment—*he was being watched.* Alika zipped up and turned slowly.

The tallest of the boys who'd attacked him stood before him. Keo's face was pale, and Alika spotted the rest of the boys hiding behind him in the undergrowth.

"Hey," he said conversationally. "You guys okay?"

"No." Keo's voice was harsh. "Someone killed the Shepherd."

"It wasn't one of you?"

"Hell, no." The boy snarled. His hands curled into fists. "We're hunting whoever did it."

"You know who it was?"

"No. Shepherd sent us out to look for food. We were panhandling on the trail. Eric went back first because he was still feeling shitty from getting in that landslide. He found the body."

Alika jerked his head in the direction of the cave. "The cops are here. They found the Shepherd. They will want to question you."

"We nevah did notting," Keo protested. "Shepherd, he was our father. We'd kill for him. We'd die for him." He drew and brandished his buck knife. It looked huge in the boy's slender hand.

"And if you run, they'll think you did it. You'll be running your whole life. Come forward. Help the cops find his killer."

Eric sidled out of the brush. The dirt cleaned from his face and body revealed a welter of bruises. The boy looked as pitiful and thin as an abused puppy as he approached Keo. "I think we should talk to the cops. We never did nothing."

"Yeah." Emilio emerged from the bushes, then Payton and finally, Raymond. The boys faced Keo in a ragtag circle. "Even if they say we did it and bust us, the worst we'd get is some time in juvie at Ko'olau." The youth correctional center on Oahu was well-known and went by the name of the valley it was nestled in. "I hear the food is okay there, and I'm sick of being hungry."

Keo slowly slid his knife back into his belt. "Okay. But if shit starts getting ugly, run for it. You all know where to go. They'll never find us if we don't want them to."

"Maybe somebody's got food now," Eric said plaintively. His ribs showed through his ripped shirt like a xylophone.

"I've got food in my chopper," Alika said. "Come with me."

He felt like the Pied Piper leading the string of boys down the trail to the helicopter parking site. He brought them straight past the backup officers milling around Nae'ole and Jenkins's helicopter over to the Dragonfly. He opened the back door and pulled out a box of water bottles and his own backpack of food supplies: beef jerky, dried fruit and coconut, some fresh wrapped cookies his grandma had made, and even a couple of SPAM musubi he hadn't had time to eat.

The boys tore into the food like wolves. Alika's chest was tight with compassion as he watched over them protectively, finally catching Jenkins's eye as the blond cop approached.

Jenkins made a beeline for Alika. The young cop kept his body language friendly, his arms relaxed, though close to his sidearm. The boys looked up warily, their cheeks bulging and muscles tense. They clustered together. Keo's hand dropped to the knife at his belt.

"Hey. Looks like you've found some of the witnesses we wanted to interview," Jenkins said casually.

"I did. These boys want to help with the investigation," Alika said. "This is Keo. He's in charge."

Jenkins stuck his hand out. "I'm Detective Jenkins with the KPD. Thanks for coming to talk to us."

The detective's friendly demeanor forced Keo to wipe a grimy hand on the back of his pants and shake. "We want to find who did it."

"That's what we're here for. I understand from Alika that you boys were camping in the cave?" Jenkins took out a small spiral pad. "Let's sit down, get comfortable. I want to take statements from each of you."

"I could use a break." Alika slammed the door of the chopper and opened a water bottle. He sat on the ground cross-legged, his back against one of the struts. "Anyone thirsty?"

Following his example, the boys were soon seated in a circle with Jenkins as Nae'ole looked on.

"We didn't know what to do," Emilio volunteered. "Keo said we should go look for who did it, because not too many people knew where we were in the cave. Just people from the camp."

"The camp?" Alika could hear the attention sharpening in Jenkins's voice, but the detective didn't look up from his note-taking. "Tell us about that."

"Nothing to do with us," Keo said sharply. "They mind their business and we mind ours."

"Let's move this along, guys. We need to speak with each of you privately. Standard operating procedure. This is Detective Nae'ole. He's going to interview you two, and I'll do you three." Jenkins stood and led Emilio off to a secluded rock outcrop, while Nae'ole took Payton over near the waterfall. Keo scowled, clearly not liking that he'd lost control of the group.

"It's going to be okay," Alika said.

"What you know?" Keo snapped, pidgin English coming out in his angry tone. "You get your own helicopter. Bruddah, you nevah been hungry."

"Maybe not. But I know shame." Alika got eye contact with the boy. "My mom had me in college, not part of anyone's plan, and my father was a *haole* guy who never owned up to it." He didn't tell many people about the wound that had led to so much angst and striving as he tried to succeed and find a place to belong as a "hapa" Caucasian and Hawaiian bastard. He'd eventually been adopted by Sean Wolcott, his mother's husband, but that hadn't happened until his teens. He was still too *haole* to be Hawaiian and too Hawaiian to be *haole*. "Everything I have, I fought for and built myself. You can too. No excuses, *bruddah*."

Keo folded his arms and looked at the ground.

The detectives continued to question the boys individually and eventually the medical examiner, a young woman with multi-colored hair, emerged from the cave.

The boys hurried to stand respectfully along the trail as the ME led the way for the police officers and crime scene investigators who carried the long, bulky, zippered black bag containing the Shepherd's body over the uneven ground to the chopper. The team loaded the body bag onto a side carry basket. The teens clustered together, clearly grieving.

"You boys should come back with us to Kapa'a," Nae'ole said. "We have a place for you to stay."

"Foster care?" Keo growled. "No thanks."

"We have a special group situation already set up for you," Jenkins said carefully. "You all get to stay together."

"So you knew about us already." Keo's accusing stare found Alika. "And you want to put us away."

"We just want you to be safe and comfortable, with food to eat and beds to sleep in," Nae'ole interjected. "Yes. Alika and his friend Sandy told us about you. That's why we came out here, to let you know about this opportunity. And then, we found the body."

Keo narrowed his eyes at Alika. "You said you wouldn't tell."

"And I didn't." Alika held the kid's eyes, trying to convey that he was keeping the secret about their attack on him. "But Sandy was under no such promise."

Jenkins's gaze flicked back and forth between them. "Speaking of Sandy. Any of you know where she's taken off to?"

The boys all shook their heads. "Never seen her."

Alika turned to them. "What do you say, guys? Shall we fly you back to Kapa'a? Ready for hot food and soft beds? Maybe even some video games?" He'd get them a game system himself if that's what it took to get them to go.

"I'll come with you." Emilio walked over to stand beside Alika. The rest of the boys did too, leaving Keo by himself. The teen scowled, indecisive, and then a shout from the direction of the trail stole all of their attention.

CHAPTER FIFTY

SOPHIE BROKE down her camp rapidly, grateful that the site had not been raided by anyone from the village. She wanted to be on the trail back to Ke'e Beach well before the first responders came to investigate the Shepherd's body. Catching her wasn't going to be a priority. Jenkins and Nae'ole would have to exit the cave where they had no signal and go back to their chopper and call for the crime scene techs and ME on the radio. They couldn't leave the body unguarded.

She had time to get away. While the detectives might want to question her for her suspicious behavior, they knew for a fact she hadn't killed the Shepherd because she'd been on Oahu and en route to Kaua'i during the murder.

As usual, the tent refused to fit into its pouch. This time Sophie didn't have time to keep redoing it, so she rolled it as tight as she could and strapped it onto the loaded backpack with a spare bungee cord. She hoisted the backpack on, tightened the straps at her hips, fastened the one at her chest, picked up her walking stick, and got moving.

Sophie and Ginger hurried up the path. She could feel the distance from Alika stretching like a fraying elastic. *She had to go faster!* Just rip away and not think about it. "Like tearing off a Band-Aid," Marcella would say.

Alika was back in her life.

In spite of everything, the knowledge was a tiny warm coal she held close. They'd rescued a boy together. They'd kissed. The feelings she'd always had for him were still there. If they hadn't broken up, that painful chapter with Connor might never have happened.

But it didn't matter. She was off men and on the run. She couldn't count on Connor's declaration that she wouldn't have any more trouble from the DA as fact. There was no room in her life for anyone but her dog.

Ginger's energy was restored by the rest and food of the last few days, and Sophie followed as the Lab galloped happily ahead of her up the narrow, boulder-strewn path.

There was simply no way to move any faster than a rapid walk hiking uphill on a rough red dirt trail, carrying a forty-pound pack on her back. She was grateful it had been dry the last couple of days; rain turned the clay-like, iron-rich soil to slick mud.

Ginger trotted just ahead, tongue lolling, as they made their way up and out of Kalalau Valley. Sophie's heart rate was up and sweat had begun to gather beneath her arms by the time they reached the first overlook outside the valley.

The view off of the rocky corner of the first switchback was breathtaking. Crenellated, green-swathed, rain-eroded ridges of coast marched away into infinity, marked by the unique shapes of *lauhala* trees, ironwoods, kukui nut and ferns. The red ribbon of pathway ran through it, zigging and zagging along the edge, inviting a journey.

Sophie found a convenient boulder and rested her pack on it, leaning forward with her hands on her knees to take in the view and catch her breath. Ginger scanned the vista at the precipitous edge of the cliff, her tail waving, and looked back at Sophie as if to confirm the beauty they were seeing.

"Yes. I know, girl. It's beautiful. But come here, away from that edge. You're making me nervous." The Lab trotted back to Sophie and sat beside her.

Clouds along the far cobalt horizon softened the endless blue as Sophie gazed without seeing, taking a moment to think through her strategy.

Hopefully, when the first responders got to the crime scene, the team would be so caught up in the investigation that they would write her off for the moment. But that outcome was unlikely in the long run. Jenkins and Nae'ole were going to assume Sophie had some inside knowledge that had led to her involvement with the lost boys; they would likely bring Alika in too, and old accusations from his past might come up.

Her identity as Sandy Mason was going to be endangered when they issued a Be On Look Out for her at the airport. She might be able to evade the cops indefinitely if she didn't try to get off the island, but without Alika's helicopter, she was stuck in Kaua'i. If she was picked up, she was going to have to reveal her identity as Sophie Ang, and if she was wanted for the murder of Assan, her next stop would be jail.

Sophie's stomach clenched at the thought and her fists balled.

It wasn't that she was afraid of being confined to a little barred box; it was the principle of the thing—Assan didn't deserve to rob her of one more day of her hard-earned life. Dead or alive, he wouldn't take anything more from her.

A rustling in nearby bushes drew her attention and Sophie's body coiled into alertness. Ginger pricked her ears. The possibilities big enough to make that degree of sound were few in Hawaii: the disturbance was likely either goat, pig, or human, and the first two stayed well away from trafficked areas, even in Kalalau.

A woman emerged from the dense foliage. Her hair was snarled into ropes, her body lank with weight loss, her clothes filthy and mud-spattered. Wild eyes fell on Sophie, and her lips drew back in a snarl.

Sophie's hands dropped to the belt at her waist and she popped the clasp, releasing the pack. Her hands flew to her chest, and she unclipped the chest strap. She was out of the confines of the backpack in seconds, letting it fall backward onto the boulder. "Enola! We found your son. He's alive!"

Enola's eyes were red-rimmed and staring. Her whole body was shaking. Enola was clearly in the ravages of shock and withdrawal. "Nakai's alive?" Her voice was a rusty hinge.

"Yes. He's in the children's hospital on Oahu." Sophie stood slowly so as not to spook the woman. "He fell into a lava tube and was trapped underground. He was injured, but he's recovering." She took a step closer to Enola. "Everyone is looking for you."

"I bet they are. And they're going to be looking harder, now." The woman held up hands crusty with dried blood in the creases. *The spatter on her dress wasn't mud.* "I haven't been much of a mother to him, but I did what I could and ended that monster when I found out what he did to those boys."

"Oh, Enola. How did you find out?"

"I went back. I caught him in his tent with one of them." She put her hands over her eyes. "The boy ran off and I went and got a rock. Did what needed to be done."

Sophie's mind buzzed. She could further the investigation by bringing in the perpetrator, and making sure Enola got the kind of legal and mental health support she obviously needed. "I can help you."

"Nakai's going to be okay?" Enola's gaze darted toward the cliff.

"Yes. He's worried about you." Sophie's brows drew together. The woman was sidling toward the precipitous overhang. "Your son's asking for you. He needs his mother."

Enola gave a bitter laugh. "It's not his job to worry about me. And now, on top of everything, he's going to have a murderer for a mother. No. I won't do that to him." She lunged for the edge with a sudden darting movement.

"No!" Sophie leaped after the woman and grabbed for her

trailing rags as Enola dove headfirst off the cliff. She barely touched the cloth of Enola's shirt and didn't even have time to close her fingers on it.

Enola plummeted out into space, arms pinwheeling, her despairing wail a ribbon of sound that would haunt Sophie's dreams.

CHAPTER FIFTY-ONE

SOPHIE TWISTED her fingers together as she sat handcuffed to the table in the Kaua'i Police Department's interview room. A hiker she'd sent back to find the detectives had brought them to the site where Enola had gone over the cliff. Sophie had waited, guarding the spot until their arrival.

She'd been arrested for obstruction of justice as soon as the detectives had arrived, and had spent an uncomfortable night in the island's general population jail cell, refusing to cooperate with questioning until her lawyer arrived from Oahu. That had delayed the interviews Nae'ole and Jenkins had tried to carry out.

The Interview Room door opened abruptly. Seeing Bennie Fernandez's cherubic white-bearded face and familiar aloha shirt made Sophie stand up, forgetting her restraints. The hard metal bracelets dug painfully into her wrists. "Mr. Fernandez! Thank you for coming."

"Of course. You're already one of my favorite clients. This is a travesty!" Fernandez exclaimed, indicating her prison orange. "Are you all right, my dear?" He patted her arm comfortingly. Sophie blinked back quick tears in response to his kindness. The depression had taken her over thoroughly, causing the last day to pass by in a blur as she lay on her back staring at the ceiling, ignoring the ebb and flow of the inmates around her.

"I am all right. I hope you brought what I asked for."

"Yes. We have a short, private consultation time before the interviews. I suggest we make the most of it. I was able to retrieve your identification from the cache where you directed me. Here it is." Fernandez opened his briefcase and slid her Sophie Ang Hawaii driver's license over to her, along with her Thailand and US passports. "I'm sure you know they are going to want answers about why you were traveling as Sandy Mason. Why was that, exactly?"

"I wanted to get away. I needed to. Somewhere beautiful, and different." Sophie touched the leatherette passport covers. The Hawaii ID, with its bright rainbow arched over her picture, looked painfully bright. Why *had* she run away as Sandy Mason? Her brain felt sluggish. *The depression.* Her medication had been confiscated along with everything else, and Ginger was currently residing in the local Humane Society. She had to get out and rescue her dog...

"That isn't going to be enough. We have to tell the detectives about the recent events involving your ex-husband. And fortunately, I have good news on that front. District Attorney Chang has completed his investigation and has decided not to proceed with any further charges against you. Assan Ang's death has been ruled self-defense."

Relief at that news made Sophie dizzy. She dropped back into her chair. "Why?"

"He faxed a statement to the effect that he'd thoroughly checked into the situation and decided that it wasn't worth the state's time to pursue a prosecution. In light of that, the HPD issued a conclusion. You're in the clear."

The door opened to admit the two detectives with their recording equipment. Jenkins was frowning. "Why didn't you just tell me you were a friend of Lei's? She called me last night and reamed me out for arresting you. You could have saved us a shitload of hassle by being up front."

Sophie dropped her eyes, spreading her fingers over the identification on the table, grounding herself with the smooth feel of the leatherette passport covers. She had no easy answer for her deception, and having been on the other side of the table, knew how it appeared.

"Let's just begin the interview properly, shall we?" Fernandez said. The detectives set up the video and audio recording equipment and Mirandized Sophie.

Jenkins seated himself. His usual energy was missing, and he rubbed a jaw bristling with blond whiskers. Nae'ole, always taciturn, glared at Sophie from beneath black brows. Jenkins opened a file. "Let's begin with your identity. State your legal name for the record, please."

"Sophie Malee Smithson Ang." Sophie pushed the pile of IDs over with the limited range allowed by the handcuffs. "I apologize for any inconvenience or misunderstanding caused by my use of an alias."

Nae'ole opened the documents and studied them as Jenkins eyed Sophie over the file. "Why don't you tell us what your purpose was in traveling under a false identity."

Sophie glanced at Fernandez. The little lawyer nodded. Sophie picked her words carefully. "I had recently been through a traumatic event and wanted to…explore the Kalalau Valley. I had an alias available through my investigation work, and I used it to travel to Kaua'i, where I became embroiled in the search for a missing boy. Things with that proceeded exactly as I first told you."

"We will get back to that and its outcome. This traumatic event. Tell us about it," Nae'ole said. The detectives' expressionless faces told Sophie they knew perfectly well what the event was.

"Let's cut to the chase," Fernandez said. "Ms. Ang killed her ex-husband in self-defense. She has been cleared of all charges in the matter." Fernandez produced a copy of the fax from the DA's office and pushed it over. The detectives examined it. "Perhaps it wasn't the wisest choice for her to leave Oahu under an alias while being investigated, but I'm sure you can empathize with the reasons. And rather than let her situation keep her from assisting in finding the missing boy, she had gone on to help in every way she could, even up to finding the boy and being trapped underground with him."

The detectives were still stony-faced, avoiding eye contact and studying the paperwork. Finally, Jenkins said, "Tell us, on the record, about your encounter with Enola Matsui."

Until this moment, Sophie hadn't heard the woman's last name. A vivid memory filled her mind: Enola's last scream, her clothing slipping through Sophie's fingers—and the sight of her body lying on the black lava rocks hundreds of feet below the trail, waves dousing it with spray.

Sophie cleared her throat. "I think it was pure chance that I saw Enola at all. She came to that high point in the trail to kill herself, and nothing I said slowed her down." She described the series of events and Enola's confession to the murder of the Shepherd. "As soon as another hiker came along, I told him to go find help and bring you back. I stayed at the site to make sure no one disturbed it or took inappropriate action."

"We only have your word for how things went down," Nae'ole said. "Maybe you pushed the victim."

"Why would I have then flagged down a hiker and sent for help, staying with the body for hours until you two arrived?"

"Because you knew you wouldn't get far once that body was discovered. Your cover identity would be blown in an even worse way than it is now," Nae'ole growled.

Sophie shrugged. "Yes. I knew I couldn't go on with the fake identity. I should have told you who I was as soon as we found the Shepherd's body and the stakes were higher. But..."

"You didn't want to go to jail for your ex's murder, no matter what the DA said," Jenkins filled in. "Lei told me a little bit of your history when she called." His clear blue gaze held compassion. "Good thing Mr. Fernandez here had the news he did, or we'd have to hold you in jail until we heard from Oahu." He pulled a photo of

Enola's sprawled, broken body out of the file and slid it over to Sophie. He pointed to a detail area showing blood spatter on her ragged gown. "The medical examiner is still doing a more in-depth analysis, but the blood type on her dress matches that of the victim. She also had blood on her hands, as you pointed out. Your story checks out."

"And what of the boys? Were they found?" Sophie asked.

"Your friend Alika was able to bring them in for questioning without incident. They all tell the same story. Those boys are kinda...Lord of the Flies." Jenkins shook his head, smiling ruefully. Sophie remembered the book from her American Literature class, and nodded as Jenkins continued. "I wouldn't want to get on their bad side in a dark alley. But with Lei's social worker friend's help, we found the perfect foster situation for them on a taro farm in Wainiha. They will stay together and live with a local family. There's a therapist visiting weekly who does *ho'oponopono*—the Hawaiian way of therapy. Hopefully the damage the Shepherd did can be undone."

"And what about Nakai?" The boy had come to mean so much to Sophie. Her chest hurt at the thought of his grief and loss. "What's happening to him?"

"He's out of the hospital, and I heard the social worker assigned to him has taken him into a foster situation with her family."

Sophie smiled in relief. "He wasn't afraid to ask for what he wanted. I am glad for him."

They hashed through a few more details and finally Fernandez stood up. "You going to let my client out of these irons? Let her get her dog out of the pound?"

"Sure thing. We're done here." Jenkins took out a key and freed Sophie from the cuffs. Rubbing her wrists, she hoped she'd never feel their cold steel again.

CHAPTER FIFTY-TWO

Several days later, Marcella watched Sophie get out of her father's shiny black Lincoln Continental in front of Marcella's cottage, carrying a white casserole dish. Frank got out of his side of the vehicle. Marcella put her hands on her hips. "And where's your potluck dish, Ambassador?"

Frank opened the back door of the Lincoln and reached in to retrieve a huge bouquet of tropical flowers. He walked up the wooden steps and handed them to Marcella. "Will these do instead?"

Burying her nose in tuberose, ginger, and sprays of orchids, Marcella nodded. "Definitely. Thanks for coming, both of you."

"I didn't think it was a choice," Sophie said. Marcella laughed and reached out to hug her friend, taking in Sophie's ashy color and sunken cheeks. Clearly her adventure in Kalalau had taken a toll.

"You're right. This is your "got out of jail free" party, and if you'd tried to stay in bed for it…well, we both know that wouldn't have worked." Marcella kissed both of Sophie's cheeks in the Italian way. "I have a surprise for you that I think will cheer you up."

Sophie managed a smile, which widened into a grin as she spotted a slender boy standing in the doorway, crutches under his arms. "Nakai!"

"Aunty Sophie!" Nakai exclaimed. At that moment, Marcella loved the Hawaiian way of expressing a relationship between a child and an adult. Frank took the casserole dish, and the normally undemonstrative Sophie ran up the wooden steps to hug the boy.

Both of them, wounded. Both of them healed in some way by the bond that had sprung up between them because of the unlikeliest of circumstances.

Marcella ushered everyone inside. She and Marcus had thrown open the slider to their backyard. Freshly mowed, with little white lights strung from the plumeria and lychee trees, the area had taken on a festive feel. Folding tables had been put together and draped in checked cloths from her parents' downtown restaurant. Her petite, busy mother Anna, bright in one of her fitted muumuus, flitted around outside setting up the food, while her papa Egidio immediately struck up a conversation with Sophie's father.

Marcella went into the kitchen and put the flowers in water, watching through the window as Sophie was greeted with hugs by Jake, Ken, and Lei, here on short notice from another case. Mrs. Feliciano, Nakai's guardian, also greeted Sophie. Marcus's sister Leolani, statuesque in a long muumuu, helped Anna with the place settings.

Marcella accepted a glass of red wine and a kiss from Marcus as he joined her. "You look beautiful," he whispered in her ear, giving her a shiver.

She kissed him back. "So do you." Her man did look scrumptious in a crisp white shirt and black jeans, his burly handsomeness set off by the simple clothing.

"I like how you bring people in and feed them. It's very Hawaiian."

"And very Italian. Who knew Hawaiians and Italians were so perfect together?"

Marcus smiled. "You read my mind as usual, and this is the perfect segue." He stepped out onto the porch, tugging Marcella by the hand. He only let go to tap his glass with a spoon. "Can I have your attention, please?"

All eyes turned toward them, and the group advanced to stand around them at the top of the porch stairs. Marcella's brows shot up in surprise as Marcus dropped to one knee before her, reaching for her hand.

"Marcella. You are the most passionate, hardworking, warm-hearted, loving, and loyal woman I've ever met. I can't imagine a better future than one spent with you, doing satisfying work together and building a life filled with friends and family. Would you do me the honor of being my wife?"

Marcella's mouth dropped open even as her eyes welled up. His speech was both smoothly delivered and heartfelt. People at HPD had always said Marcus Kamuela could sell refrigerators to Eskimos, and her frozen shock began to melt as he turned to their friends. "I think I surprised her." A rustle of nervous laughter passed through the group as Marcella closed her mouth with an effort. Marcus took out a small black velvet box. "A tiny token of my love for you. I'd be the happiest man in the world if you'd wear it."

The massive diamond solitaire ring resting on a black velvet cushion was hardly tiny—it was at least a couple of carats. Ridiculous. Over the top. Totally impractical. Just like Marcus to get her something a movie star would wear.

"Holy crap!" Marcella clapped her hands over her mouth as her tears overflowed. Marcus stayed on bended knee as she scolded, "You brat! I can't believe you sprang this on me, and this rock! You could have gotten a new car!" She plucked the diamond out of the box and slid it on, throwing her arms around his solid body and bending to kiss him in a frenzy. "Yes, Marcus, yes! Of course I'll marry you!"

Cheers, applause, and laughter swirled around them like bubbles in champagne, but all Marcella noticed were her beloved's arms around her as he rose to crush her tight in the longest hug.

CHAPTER FIFTY-THREE

Sᴏᴘʜɪᴇ'ꜱ ᴇʏᴇꜱ burned as she watched the tender scene play out on the porch between Marcella and Marcus. Her heart was so full of joy —she was watching a fairy tale come true. *Maybe love between a man and a woman really could work.* There was no darkness in the beauty she was witnessing: only light, and love, and honesty.

But not for her. Never for her. She'd been broken one too many times.

When Marcus stood and drew his fiancée into his arms for a hug, Sophie finally blinked. Tears rolled down her cheeks, hot and unwelcome.

"Are you okay?" Jake was standing beside her—she'd forgotten he was there. His whisper raised the hairs on the back of her neck. He took her nerveless, cold hand in one of his.

"I'm just so happy for them." Sophie removed her hand. *She didn't deserve to be touched, to be warm.* Her feet were too far away, her vision telescoping. She heard words in her head, spoken in Dr. Wilson's voice, but they came out in her own. "A dissociative episode is occurring."

"What?" Jake stepped in front of her. He loomed, filling her vision, blocking the view of her friends. His big hands gripped her shoulders. "Sit down."

He physically moved her stiff, unresponsive form over to a chair under the plumeria tree and pushed her down into it. "You need a drink." He disappeared.

Sophie sat, completely isolated from what was happening. Her body felt inanimate, a robot that contained her essence as she observed the exclaiming chaos that followed the proposal, the toasts led by Egidio, the radiant smile Marcella flashed at the group as she held up her hand with the dazzling ring on it, her face alight with happiness and shiny with tears as Marcus squeezed her against his side.

Seated in the shadows under the plumeria tree out of view, Sophie just breathed, trapped in her body— and gradually her atoms reassembled themselves. One by one, Sophie's senses seemed to reboot, drawing her back into the here and now.

She smelled the fresh-cut grass and the tree overhead. She heard the Hawaiian music and the joyful explosion of congratulations going on. She felt the plastic arms of the chair under her hands, the way the evening air wafted across her freshly shaved legs in Mary Watson's flowered skirt. She saw the beauty and love before her. She smiled, and felt her cheeks move.

Jake reappeared with a couple of glasses of champagne. "Here. Toast." He stood beside her and she lifted her glass as Frank stepped up to lead another toast to the happy couple.

Sophie sipped the sparkling wine at the toast. She tasted its tartness, felt the bubbles in her nose, at the back of her throat. She swallowed the last of her tears down, down, down, into the darkness inside of her. And she closed the lid on it, for now.

"I'm okay. I'm okay now, Jake." She smiled up at him. "Thanks. I just needed a moment. And a glass of champagne." She glanced over at the porch.

Marcella was looking for her, scanning the party area, a crease between her brows.

Her friend would be worried, wanting Sophie to be okay, instinctively concerned about how her own good fortune would affect her unlucky friend. *Marcella was that kind of person.*

Sophie didn't deserve Marcella's friendship, but she had to get past herself to do right by it. She knew that much. She stood up, handed her champagne glass to Jake, and strode across the grass and up the stairs to engulf both Marcus and Marcella in her biggest, best, strongest hug. "I am so happy for you two. You give me hope," she said into the sweet space between their faces.

And in that moment, it was true.

THE GHOST RAN along the night beach, the weight of his Walther PPK in the shoulder harness smacking lightly against his ribs. He didn't find the reminder of his weapon annoying any longer—he'd been wearing it so constantly that it had become a part of him, an extension like the dog at his side.

Anubis was off leash, trotting on sand so white and fine it reminded him of sugar, gleaming silver under the stars. Here in Thailand, no leash rules bound them but Anubis's training.

Delicate moonlit ripples splashed onto the shore, glowing blue with bioluminescence. The dark shapes of unfamiliar tropical trees and tiny offshore islands created an exotic moonlit vista. The Ghost remembered Hawaii with a pang; this was just as beautiful, but he missed Sophie's presence as she ran with him, that lovable, unmannerly dog of hers romping ahead.

Sophie should come home to Thailand and sort out her relationship with her mother. Make peace with her past. It would be good for her to deal with those old wounds, and Thailand was a place where she'd blend in beautifully.

He allowed himself a fantasy of the life they could have far from the restrictions and prying eyes of her law enforcement background.

Perhaps Sophie would reach out to him through the software

program, or the chat room they had set up and used in the past. *He was a patient man.* Someday she would forgive him, and they would have the future he longed for.

For now, Thailand was rife with corruption and needed the Ghost's full attention.

CHAPTER FIFTY-FOUR

SOPHIE SETTLED herself into the now-familiar seat in the Bell Jet Ranger. Seated beside her, Alika handed her a helmet and she slipped it on, clipping the chinstrap and turning on the comm unit.

"Ready?" Alika's warm brown eyes gleamed behind his face visor.

"Ready." Sophie gave a thumbs-up.

Alika hit the ignition switch, and the chopper thrummed to life.

It had been two weeks since Sophie returned to Oahu and the case in Kalalau wrapped up. She and Ginger had spent that time at her father's apartment recuperating: resuming her workouts at the new gym, Fighting Fit, catching up with her friends, and figuring out her next steps.

Security Solutions had offered to extend her private security contract, but she had declined for the moment. Now that the oppressive pall of possible charges against her had lifted, Sophie wanted to continue her exploration of the Hawaiian Islands on foot.

Alika, on Oahu to check in with his gym, had offered to fly her to her next destination, the Big Island. Sophie wanted to hike the many trails of that splendid and primordial island after a stop to visit with Dr. Caprice Wilson in Hilo. She was looking forward to seeing the petite blonde psychologist again, and having someone she knew and trusted help her sort through the threads of her life.

Alika lifted the collective, and the helicopter rose as gently as if floating. Sophie sucked in a breath of awe and exhilaration as the chopper soared off of her father's high-rise building and veered over the downtown Honolulu skyline.

Early morning sun gilded the east side of the skyscrapers, lighting the waves far below, already dotted with surfers in the Waikiki lineup. The helicopter tilted as they headed south, and Sophie turned her head to bid the rugged silhouette of Diamond Head, site of many of her run-hikes, goodbye.

They left the city behind. Sophie scanned the crinkled blue surface of the ocean for whale signs as her hand crept back to caress Ginger's big square head. The Lab was tied behind her seat for safety, but had wedged herself as far forward as she could get, her muzzle aligned with Sophie's thigh.

The wind was not yet up, making the flight smooth. They passed the great yellow and green hump that was Maui, and soon they were circling in to fly low over glowing red veins of trickling lava making their way through a vast blackened plain. She'd asked Alika to take her to where the flows from Kilauea Volcano met the sea on an area of newborn land. It had seemed a good place to start her latest journey.

Alika searched for a smooth landing spot, and finally set the Dragonfly down on the last bit of paved road in Kalapana, before it was buried in hardened coruscations of black stone.

He removed his helmet and Sophie hers as the rotors slowed and the engine whined to a stop. She took a thick wad of cash out of her pocket and held it out to him. "For expenses."

Alika shook his head. "No need."

"Yes. There is a need. I have taken your time and used your equipment. You must be compensated."

Alika's golden-brown gaze met hers. He reached over and hooked a hand around the back of her neck, drawing her toward him.

Sophie's eyes closed and she sank into the kiss. A long moment passed as they savored the taste and touch of each other.

She drew back into her seat. Her hand touched her tingling lips.

"All I need by way of compensation." Alika said.

Her cheeks heated. She looked away. "I can't be in a relationship right now."

"I understand. I know you need time to recover from everything. Time to learn there are still people you can trust. I just want to be one of those."

Sophie looked down and thought of Jake.

She missed Jake. He had been back on the Maui job after Marcella's engagement party, and they'd had no contact other than a few phone calls. Jake was someone she could trust. So were Marcella and Lei. Even Waxman and Ken Yamada were people she could trust— and her father, back at his ambassador job in Washington, most of all.

Sophie was surrounded by an "*ohana*" of friends and family. This journey she was on still needed to be taken alone, but a tiny flame of hope rose in her that it wouldn't always be that way.

Alika got out of his side of the chopper, and as he turned away, Sophie slid the money into a slot beside his seat. *Better not to make any unspoken promises she couldn't keep.*

She led Ginger out through her passenger door as Alika lifted out her heavy backpack and set it on the road. He looked around. "No one anywhere for miles out here. I feel bad just letting you out like this. You sure you don't need a ride somewhere?"

Sophie smiled. "I am fully capable of making my own way anywhere I want to go. Thank you for all you've done. I'll be in touch."

"You better be. Or I'll come looking for you." Alika smiled, but she knew he meant it.

She watched as the helicopter lifted off of the lava and into the sky, buzzing away like the dragonfly he'd named it.

Sophie hefted the backpack and shrugged into it, settling the weight on her hips. It was full of camping and food supplies, and she made sure that the side pocket containing the Ghost software and her satellite laptop with DAVID loaded on it was specially waterproofed and travel ready. She'd also brought her Glock this time, since she was traveling under her own name with a concealed carry permit, and wouldn't be taking a commercial airline flight.

Sophie tightened the straps, picked up Ginger's leash, and headed into the virgin lava field, a feeling a lot like joy filling her with strength for the journey ahead, wherever it might lead.

Turn the page for a sneak peek of book six of the Paradise Crime Thrillers, *Wired Justice*!

SNEAK PEEK

WIRED JUSTICE, PARADISE CRIME THRILLERS BOOK 6

The best place to think about life was on a volcano. Sophie tried to hold that thought as she held a hand up to shade her eyes. Alika Wolcott, ex-coach and possible lover, had piloted the chopper that had dropped her off in this desolate lava field, and now she was on her own hiking adventure with her faithful dog, Ginger.

Kalapana on the Big Island was a place of stark contrasts. The deep blue sky arced overhead, depthless and unbroken. Desolate as a moonscape, acres of black lava, some areas barely cooled, stretched away in every direction to the ocean, where a restless sea beat against the fresh stone. The only sign of human presence was the remains of what had once been a two-lane highway, engulfed periodically by shiny black rock that gleamed iridescent in the sun of high noon.

"Come, Ginger." The dog had been nosing for smells around a rock, and came to Sophie's side. Sophie attached the Lab's leash to her belt with a clip and tightened the straps of her backpack once more, settling the weight so it rested evenly on her hips. She set off toward the area of active flow that she had been able to see from the chopper.

A road of sorts had been made across the fresh stone by all the tourists visiting the lava flow area. It was easy to follow their tracks, and as the morning wore on, she encountered people riding rented bikes, other hikers, and tourists of every stripe, age, and build. A quad even rumbled past her, towing a flat trailer loaded with tourists.

Sophie reached a crude viewing area taped off with yellow caution tape and found a good vantage point, slightly out of the gusty wind that whipped over the wide flank of the volcano, hitting the ocean like a cat batting with its paw. The lava ran in a sinuous, slow moving, hypnotic glowing river to the edge of the cliff. Molten, glowing chunks dropped into the sea in a relentless stream, causing explosions of steam and a crackling sound like breaking glass as extreme heat met its match.

Sophie watched from beside a stone bulwark, one hand on Ginger's ruff. The dog whined in excitement, but calmed under her hand. Hours passed with no sense of time as Sophie watched the blood of the land ooze forth, hit the water in sizzling bursts, and slowly and inexorably build the island.

Sunset came spectacularly. The tourists mounted their bikes, shouldered their toddlers, and headed back to the parking area some miles away. Sophie ate an energy bar and fed Ginger her kibble, still watching the lava trickle into the sea, the glow brightening as darkness fell. She felt no urgency to leave or do anything more. *This was all, and it was enough.*

The stars came out and the moon rose. Sophie undid her bedroll and sleeping bag and lay down with her dog close against her, and her eyes on the lava's pageantry.

The soft breath of the morning breeze caressed Sophie's face, waking her. She had come to no conclusions nor had any deep insights, lying there on the cliff and watching the lava drip into the ocean—but she reveled in that elusive sense of freedom she'd been seeking. She finally rolled up her sleeping bag and headed out.

She didn't feel ready to deal with people right now, and was glad of the early morning emptiness of the area. Off in the nearby ocean as she and Ginger walked over the raw lava, she glimpsed a whale spout.

Ginger was off leash, and the dog gave a sudden bark, signaling her interest in something, and lunged off of the foot path worn over the fresh stone. Sophie grabbed for her collar, but the Lab galloped away across the rough surface.

"Ginger, no!" Sophie cried, worried that the dog's feet would be cut on the razor-sharp lava. "Ginger, come!" She scrambled after the Lab, continuing to call as she ran as fast as her forty-pound pack would allow. *Ginger could be impulsive, but this level of disobedience was rare.* Sophie finally dropped the backpack to gain speed in running after the dog. "Ginger!"

The Lab seemed to be heading for a stand of burned trees, emerging like an island in a sea of black lava. Sophie had heard that these protrusions of unburned land were called *kipukas.* She scowled with fear and concern, noticing steam wafting up from cracks. They were running around on an active hot zone!

Ginger disappeared into a stand of hardy ohia trees marking the edge of the *kipuka.* Sophie, a few minutes behind, entered the sheltering trees, her heart pounding with anxiety and frustration. "Ginger! Bad dog! You are not getting off the leash anymore!"

The dog's answer was a sharp yap, followed by a frantic whine.

Something was wrong.

Sophie crashed through brittle underbrush, swatting aside branches.

The sweet, rotting smell of decomposition hit Sophie's nose: *of course!* Ginger was so excited about some awful dead animal. Nothing made the dog happier then rolling in a nicely aged piece of roadkill. She had to catch the damn dog before she rolled in whatever had drawn her all this way.

Sophie parted the branches of a hardy guava tree, and stopped short with a gasp.

Ginger stood, tail waving, amid a pile of dead bodies.

Jake Dunn prided himself on his focus. Yeah, people said he was impulsive, but they just didn't understand how he worked. He followed his gut. When he got an idea, "just do it" was his motto. He'd seldom been wrong in these "impulses."

And now, his gut told him that something smelled fishy on the Big Island.

Security Solutions' newest clients, a couple in their early sixties wearing the golf shirts and chinos of the well-to-do, sat in chairs across from Jake and his boss, Acting President of Operations Kendall Bix.

Bix was taking their information. "So how long has your daughter been missing?"

"Two weeks." Kent Weathersby spoke, petting his wife's hand over and over. Jake's skin crawled, imagining how that must feel, but the woman seemed to find it comforting. She snuggled into her husband, her immaculately coiffed head nestled on his shoulder. "We reported Julie missing after she didn't check in with us for our scheduled talk. She had been on a backpacking trip through the islands, and we'd agreed she would check in with us weekly. She's been on the Big Island a week when we stopped hearing from her. It's been two since she disappeared. The Hilo police department closest to the area where she was last seen has not been able to find her."

Weathersby spoke mechanically, as if he had rehearsed the speech so it would flow smoothly, even as his wife, Betty, winced visibly with each mention of their daughter's disappearance. Tears oozed out from under her lids.

Jake cleared his throat. "I hope we can be of help, but you understand we will need to work closely with local law enforcement, and not step on anyone's toes or duplicate efforts on the investigation."

Sergeant Lei Texeira, a Maui Police Department detective, was a friend who had begun her career on the Big Island. It might be worth getting in touch to make some connections to smooth the way, and ask for backstory on the case.

"Julie usually found a group of other campers to hang out with both for safety and fun. She was camping outside Volcanoes National Park when she disappeared. We don't know if she found anyone to hang out with yet." Betty's wet blue eyes in her softly wrinkled face found Jake's, and brought on a twinge of guilt. *She reminded him of his mom.*

His mom had flown all the way from Texas to be at his bedside when he was recovering from a recent gunshot wound. His sisters had also come over. Totally unnecessary, but at least they'd all been able to get a Hawaii vacation out of it. Jake's gaze strayed to the windows, where he could see a sliver of ocean in the distance between the buildings.

The ocean was his favorite thing about living in Honolulu. It made him feel free. *But it was just an illusion.* He'd never been free —never would be. Wherever he went, there he was, carrying his chains of obligation.

"I think we should be able to get some more answers for you," Bix said. "Two weeks isn't long to be missing for a young woman of your daughter's age. She probably met a guy and…you know." Bix smiled. The expression sat uneasily on his stern mouth as if perched there.

"We've been getting that same feeling from the police department that you're giving us now: they don't take us seriously. They think our daughter is shacked up with some man, living off the grid. That's the message we've been getting over and over. But our Julie is not like that," Weathersby said starkly. "Something's happened. Something's wrong."

Jake slapped his thighs and stood up. "I believe you. I'll go to the Big Island and find her." He turned to look at Bix. "And I know just the woman to help. Our rogue agent, Sophie Ang."

Download *Wired Justice* and continue reading now!

ACKNOWLEDGMENTS

Aloha dear readers!

I'm so excited. Sophie is on her way in a whole new direction as an independent crime solver, armed with DAVID and the Ghost software. She's a "female Jack Reacher," but with a backpack and a lot of friends and a good dog by her side. I can't wait to see what she gets up to next!

This book is written in a new style, with brief chapters and several points of view. I'm always trying to surprise and intrigue you readers with new approaches, and I hope this latest journey worked for you.

Several years ago, I was intrigued by an article about a rogue group of campers squatting way back in Kalalau Valley, and the efforts by rangers and the DLNR to get them out. Not long after, I heard of a female hiker who was murdered, thrown off the trail to her death. I decided then and there I'd be using that gorgeous, remote, *mana*-infused valley for a story.

Growing up on Kaua'i, our family hiked to Hanakapiai on a regular basis and took a little wooden boat with an outboard all the way to Kalalau to camp when I was a kid. A great way to see Kalalau's unforgettable majesty is from the top at the Koke'e lookout. The view down the valley to the sea is one of the most beautiful in the world.

I took artistic license with the occurrence of lava tubes in Kalalau. These most likely do not exist in this particular location, so no unauthorized waterfall spelunking on my book info!

Thanks go out to my awesome copyeditors Don and Bonnie, who try valiantly to get the Paradise Crime books in shape for my typo hunters Shirley and Angie. Thanks also to my faithful, hardworking Tricia and creative new helper Jamie, for all your PR efforts. I appreciate everyone on my team, and couldn't do all this without you.

Special love and kisses to my husband Mike as the two of us embark on a new chapter of our lives, living in California for a season on the Russian River. Until next time, I'll be writing! Keep reading for an excerpt from Wired Justice, Paradise Crime #6.

Much aloha,

FREE BOOKS

Join my mystery and romance lists and receive free, full-length, award-winning novels *Torch Ginger & Somewhere on St. Thomas.*

tobyneal.net/TNNews

TOBY'S BOOKSHELF

PARADISE CRIME SERIES

Paradise Crime Mysteries
Blood Orchids
Torch Ginger
Black Jasmine
Broken Ferns
Twisted Vine
Shattered Palms
Dark Lava
Fire Beach
Rip Tides
Bone Hook
Red Rain
Bitter Feast

Paradise Crime Mystery
Special Agent Marcella Scott
Stolen in Paradise

Paradies Crime Suspense Mysteries
Unsound

Paradise Crime Thrillers
Wired In
Wired Rogue
Wired Hard
Wired Dark
Wired Dawn
Wired Justice
Wired Secret
Wired Fear
Wired Courage
Wired Truth

ROMANCES

The Somewhere Series
Somewhere on St. Thomas
Somewhere in the City
Somewhere in California

Standalone
Somewhere on Maui

Co-Authored Romance Thrillers
The Scorch Series
Scorch Road
Cinder Road
Smoke Road
Burnt Road
Flame Road
Smolder Road

YOUNG ADULT

<u>Standalone</u>
Island Fire

NONFICTION

<u>Memoir</u>
Freckled

ABOUT THE AUTHOR

Kirkus Reviews calls Neal's writing, *"persistently riveting. Masterly."*

Award-winning, USA Today bestselling social worker turned author Toby Neal grew up on the island of Kaua`i in Hawaii. Neal is a mental health therapist, a career that has informed the depth and complexity of the characters in her stories. Neal's mysteries and thrillers explore the crimes and issues of Hawaii from the bottom of the ocean to the top of volcanoes. Fans call her stories, *"Immersive, addicting, and the next best thing to being there."*

Neal also pens romance, romantic thrillers, and writes memoir/non-fiction under TW Neal.

Visit tobyneal.net for more ways to stay in touch!
or
Join my Facebook readers group, *Friends Who Like Toby Neal Books,* for special giveaways and perks.

Made in the USA
Coppell, TX
05 October 2020

39317971R00152